Terror on Every Side!

THE LIFE OF JEREMIAH

VOLUME 4

The Darkness Deepens

Mark Morgan

Bible
Tales
www.BibleTales.online

Published in Australia by Bible Tales Online.
www.BibleTales.online

**Terror on Every Side! The Life of Jeremiah
Volume 4 – The Darkness Deepens**

ISBN (Paperback): 978-1-925587-03-6
ISBN (eBook): 978-1-925587-13-5

Last updated: 24 December 2019.

Cover picture: Jerusalem from the Mount of Olives by Frederick Edwin Church (1870).

Free Download

Paul in Snippets

A 109-page PDF novelette by Mark Morgan.

The life of Paul painted from the Acts of the Apostles.

Get your free copy of *Paul in Snippets* when you sign up for the Bible Tales mailing list. As well as the eBook, you will receive a weekly email newsletter with micro tales, informative articles and special offers.

Visit **http://www.BibleTales.online/free-pins**

www.BibleTales.online

To my ever-patient wife, Ruth.

Acknowledgements and thanks

In 2014, I prompted my daughter Heidi to write a Bible-based story. Her response was that I should show her how! This is my attempt to do so.

Particular thanks go to Ruth, my wife, who helped me find time to write, patiently read what I wrote, and humoured me when I spent inordinate amounts of time on research into minute details.

Feedback from early readers and subscribers has improved the story greatly, so I thank them. No manuscript is ever without errors, but these early readers helped eliminate most typos, bad grammar and uncomfortable usage. Cathy, my oldest daughter has tirelessly undertaken the thankless task of proof reading the entire manuscript more than once. Thanks, Cathy.

My son Chris has also helped with various technical details and his excellent reading has made the audio book a pleasure to listen to. I never expected to enjoy listening to anything I had written, but Chris achieved this.

A request

I have a request to make of all readers: if you find any errors; typos, spelling errors, poor grammar, unkempt use of vocabulary, or, most importantly, errors of fact where the story misrepresents the Bible, please let me know. I can't correct printed books, but electronic versions and any new printed editions can be fixed.

VOLUME FOUR

The Darkness Deepens

Contents

"Terror on Every Side!"

For I hear the whispering of many—
terror on every side!—
as they scheme together against me,
as they plot to take my life.

A psalm of David: Psalm 31:13

For I hear many whispering.
Terror is on every side!
"Denounce him! Let us denounce him!"
say all my close friends,
watching for my fall.
"Perhaps he will be deceived;
then we can overcome him
and take our revenge on him."

Jeremiah 20:10

Chapter 1

Besieged

December, 598 BC – the 1st year of King Jeconiah

The biting cold – and the need to remain unseen – both kept me huddled behind a small tree. The lashing rain made me reflect wistfully on comfortable evenings spent around a warm fire.

Not far from me, a sizzling watch-fire flickered and sputtered as the gusts of wind and rain threatened to completely overwhelm the timid flames. Ample fuel lay within reach of the blaze, but the drenching rain was winning.

Reluctant guards tended the fire, paying little attention to any possible threat of danger. After all, who would be out on a night like this?

It was late on a winter's night and I was hiding near the top of the pass between the Mount of Olives and the

Mount of Watchmen[1] – though little could be seen of any watchmen that night! A multitude of lights marked the locations of Chaldean camp fires around Jerusalem, but the lights often glimmered feebly or vanished completely behind the windblown rain that periodically reduced visibility to almost nothing.

Nebuchadnezzar's army surrounded Jerusalem, preventing any from coming or going, patiently and methodically strangling the life from a beleaguered city in which supplies, once used, could not be replaced.

On this particular winter's night, however, Nebuchadnezzar's soldiers were concentrating on themselves. For all they cared, an entire army could come or go as it pleased, as long as they did not have to expose themselves to the ferocious wind and periodic sleet. A winter storm was spending its fury on the city and its encircling enemies, and none would be so foolish as to brave the elements. None, I thought, except for me.

As I had travelled cautiously south from the Euphrates River, news had reached me about the Chaldean army's siege of Jerusalem. Rumours suggested that King Jehoiakim had been captured or injured, but no-one could confirm their truth.

God had given me a message for the king and his mother. At the time I did not understand why the message would be for Jehoiakim's mother, as she was not in favour with her wayward son. However, God's word must be delivered, so here I was, hidden high on an exposed hill seeking a way to enter a city under siege. If I was to succeed, this was just the weather I needed.

It was time to change the guards, and the fortunate guards whose watch was over retired into the relative

---

[1] Har Hatsophim (הַר הַצּוֹפִים), also called Mount Scopus, is to the north of, and slightly taller than, the Mount of Olives.

comfort of their flapping tent. No doubt they would do their best to get warm, clapping and stamping, trying to restore feeling to their numbed fingers and toes. One unlucky guard remained outside on watch, single-handedly protecting this extremity of an army camped uncomfortably far from their homes.

Gingerly, I crept out from behind the tree, crouching low as I sneaked past the fire with its sole guard and continued the risky task of making my way towards the walls of Jerusalem. As I went and the weather continued to worsen, it became increasingly clear that the risk was not great. Very few people were moving along the road that led towards the Benjamin Gate. On an ordinary night, I'm sure that the guards stationed near the fires beside the track would have been accosting any traveller who dared to pass, but on this night, the guards remained huddled near fires that struggled even to stay alight, and any foolhardy soul who trod the road did so unquestioned.

One or two hardy travellers passed me in the windy darkness, their cloaks wrapped tightly around them to hide even their faces from any passing inspection. Could it be that they too did not want to be known? It occurred to me that I might not be the only one seeking entry to or egress from the city under the cover of a wild and frigid darkness. The thought filled me with hope. I hurried towards the gate, with one last camp fire to pass – a larger blaze, several hundred metres from the wall. More guards were huddled around it, too. As I approached, though, a particularly strong flurry of sleet and icy rain blew across the road, causing the guards to huddle even more closely behind their shields, their hooded cloaks wrapped tightly around them. I slipped past, unseen.

The road between there and the city wall was completely devoid of light, and I was glad that I was familiar with the terrain, although the unaccustomed heavy rainfall made the road slippery and difficult. There were also unexpected obstacles on the road, and I stumbled and almost fell a few times. Finally, it occurred to me that the Chaldeans might have deliberately placed barriers on the road to slow down any attacks that might come from the gate, and from then on I moved more cautiously. It was far too dark to see the things I had been tripping over, so all I could do was to hold my hands out in front of me and edge my way forward.

As I neared the brooding bulk of the stone archway of the Benjamin Gate, the city wall gradually began to offer a little protection from the elements. Eventually I reached the gatehouse with its vaulted roof and massive stone walls which created a protected area immediately in front of the large wooden gates. I stood for a moment enjoying the comparative warmth, but there was no time to waste. Somehow, I must get the attention of the men in the city without exciting any suspicion that I was an enemy.

Being out of the storm gave me the chance to notice how much I was shivering and just how cold the rain dripping from the end of my nose was. The night was still getting colder, and even under the shelter of the gate, my teeth were chattering so loudly that it seemed as though the Chaldean soldiers must surely be able to hear them!

I raised my fist and banged on the gate. Three, four, five times. Then I listened carefully. No response, so after a while, I banged again, for longer this time. Once again I waited, looking back anxiously towards the nearest campfire. Surely they must be able to hear all the noise I was making? But the howling wind was still whipping the sleet and rain across the road, and the closest Chaldean guard post was almost invisible.

Yet again, I struck the gate as firmly as I could, ten or twelve times, until finally I heard a faint voice from behind the gate, almost completely masked by the roar of the wind behind me. "Someone's knocking," said the muffled voice, and I heaved a sigh of relief. Step one had been completed. Now to see whether they would let me in. How could I convince them that I was a lone Hebrew and not leading an attacking force of Chaldean soldiers?

Suddenly a voice came from above my head. "Who are you?"

"I am Jeremiah, the son of Hilkiah," I replied, looking up, but unable to see anything that showed where the voice was coming from.

"Move back a few steps from the gate," said the voice, and I obeyed.

A very small hatch in one of the massive wooden doors opened and a light was held up behind it. Some of the light shone through the hole and illuminated my face, and I pushed the hood back from my face so that it could be seen as clearly as possible in the dim and flickering light.

"Ah," said the voice from above, "you really could be Jeremiah, though you look more like a drowned rat at the moment!"

"Yes, I am Jeremiah and I want to come in," I said.

"Everyone else is trying to get out; why do you want to come in?" came the disembodied voice again, but by that time I had seen a small aperture in the vaulted roof above me. It had obviously been included at the time when the gate was built for just such a purpose as this, so that the guards could see what was happening outside the gate, without themselves being in danger, or being seen.

"I have a message from Yahweh for the king," I replied, deliberately avoiding naming the king until I could find out what the truth was.

"Does delivering your message include bringing Chaldean soldiers into the city?"

"What do you mean?" I asked.

"Are you working for the king of Babylon as some people say?"

"I work for Yahweh the God of Israel, not for any king," I answered, suddenly feeling very tired and starting to worry that the Chaldeans might take an interest in the activity in the gateway. Would they be able to see the light that shone through the small hole in the gate? "There are no Chaldean soldiers with me or near me. Not yet. But if we keep talking for too long, that might change," I insisted, urgently. "Can you please hurry up and let me in?"

A different voice answered me from above, saying, "You can come in, but be very careful. Don't make any sudden movements or turn round at all, or make any signals. When the gate opens, just walk forward quickly and silently. Then we can find out whether you really are Jeremiah or not."

"Alright," I said, and waited.

A few moments later, I heard the sounds of heavy wooden bars being moved behind the gate. This seemed to last for an interminable time, but I obeyed the orders I had been given and continued to face directly towards the gate. It was a frightening wait, knowing that any manner of death could be approaching silently from behind and I would know nothing of it. Eventually, one of the gates swung open a short way and I walked smartly into Jerusalem. Immediately the gate was slammed behind me and men started lifting the heavy bars swiftly into place again. Four guards were standing just inside the gate with spears levelled at me, their sharp points unpleasantly close to my dripping cloak. Behind them, another four guards stood with their swords ready, just in case. The movement of heavy pieces of timber continued behind me, and I turned to see that there were many more bars across the gate than was normal. They must have been put in place to keep out the Chaldeans. It was clear that the city was taking the siege seriously.

My shivering was now completely uncontrollable, and I could hardly talk as relief overcame me. The chief of the night guard came down from the tower and began to question me. One of the guards put down his sword and began to search me thoroughly. I tried to explain my presence, while rainwater dripped from my clothes and hair, forming a spreading puddle around my feet.

For some time, the captain was very suspicious, as he could not see any good reasons why a friend would try to enter a besieged city. My explanation that I had work to do for Yahweh clearly sounded incredible in his ears, and I could not offer any other explanation. For him and his men, Jerusalem was a city of fear and hopelessness. It was plain that they would never have tried to get in again if opportunity had placed them safely outside the walls. Their attitude brought home to me the danger of the situation I had chosen. What would happen to me when the siege inevitably ended and Jerusalem was destroyed?

Finally, they decided to find some other way to verify my identity. Wearily, I put my dripping hood back over my head and was led through the slowly moderating storm to the house of the High Priest, Azariah. By that time I was feeling very old, desperate to find somewhere to lie down, and uncertain whether I would ever be able to get warm again. Every step was exhausting. As we arrived at the High Priest's house and saw a feeble light shining from inside, the captain heaved a sigh of relief. He was not completely convinced about me, but he would not have dared to disturb the High Priest's repose to ask for a final identification of this bedraggled refugee who had blown onto their doorstep in a winter storm. I have no doubt that without some confirmation of my identity, I would have spent the rest of the night in a dark cell, possibly freezing to death.

One of Azariah's servants opened the door and the captain of the guard explained apologetically that he was sorry for the lateness of the hour but that he needed to see the High Priest right away to confirm a man's identity. The servant looked at me, but clearly did not recognise me in the dark and wearing a hood. As we waited, I removed the dripping hood once more to make sure that there would be no question about my identity.

Azariah came to the door carrying a lamp, with the servant following behind and peering over his shoulder, obviously intrigued by these late-night events.

"What do you want?" asked my brother, sounding a little grumpy at this interruption to his personal time. Then he raised his lamp so that the dim light fell upon my face as I stood a little behind the captain of the guard. "You!" he said in surprise, and not altogether happily. "We thought you were off wandering somewhere in the north. What made you come back? More trouble to tell us about?"

"Excuse me," interrupted the captain before I could answer. "You are Azariah, the son of Hilkiah, aren't you? The High Priest of Yahweh?" He spoke formally, probably in an attempt to avoid the family quarrel he sensed brewing.

"Yes, I am," replied Azariah. "Who are you?"

"I am Telah, the captain of the guard at the Benjamin Gate. This man came seeking entry to the city a few minutes ago."

"What, in this weather?" Azariah asked, looking at me.

"I couldn't get to the gates at all in any other weather," I said, wearily.

"I suppose not. But I'm surprised that anyone is seriously guarding the gate in such a storm."

"We must still guard the gates even in this weather, sir. Jerusalem must be protected," the captain said virtuously. "Anyway, this man claims to be your brother, Jeremiah, the son of Hilkiah. Can you please identify him for me so that I can get back to my post?"

Azariah looked at me and for a moment I wondered whether he was considering denying that he knew me, but it probably never even occurred to him – he never had much of a sense of humour, and the importance of his position had made him even more serious over the years. It was certainly good for me on that particular night.

"Yes," he answered, slowly. "Yes, he is indeed Jeremiah, the son of Hilkiah. I vouch for him."

"Very well then: he is free to go." He looked at me with sympathy, and then spoke to Azariah confidingly, "But, he's a bit of a drowned rat at the moment, sir – and a very cold one at that. Well, good night." He nodded at Azariah, and then at me, then walked off into the night, back towards the gate.

Azariah looked at me again and shook his head. "What am I going to do with you, Jeremiah?" he asked, sounding a lot like our father for a few moments.

"Is our mother in Jerusalem?" I asked, changing the subject. I was cold, but I also wanted to get some answers before finding somewhere to get warm and dry.

"Yes," replied Azariah, "she has been staying with us since a week before the siege began."

"Did she come because she heard news that they were on the way?"

"No. It's hard to believe, but no-one in the city knew they were coming until the vanguard was seen by a few on the slopes of Har Hatsophim," answered Azariah.

"Which just goes to show how much people believe the word of God!" I said bitterly, still shivering as the puddles around my sodden sandals continued to widen.

"Yes, well, we won't go into that," said Azariah. "We need to make sure that you have somewhere to stay. Where did you plan to stay tonight?" He looked at me closely and seemed to actually notice my windswept and wet appearance for the first time. "You look cold." A masterful understatement, that. "We have a spare room where you can stay. If you don't get out of those clothes soon, we might have another casualty to add to the already long list. Come in, come in!"

He stood aside and waved me in through the doorway. The servant was still standing behind him, and Azariah said, "Rei, Jeremiah needs to get dry and warm." He looked at me as I shuffled past him, still dripping and now shivering uncontrollably once more. I thought of the fine rugs in many of the rooms of the house and wondered whether the same thoughts were occurring to Azariah. "Heat up some water and then take him into the washing room," continued Azariah. "Get him some clothes and whatever he needs to get dry. In the meantime, while you are heating the water, he can come into the scroll room and warm up a bit in front of the fire – there are no rugs on the floor in there. Do you need any food, Jeremiah?"

"I haven't eaten since this morning. There were lots of soldiers around Anathoth and I wasn't sure if it was safe to be seen there. I found out that mother was not at our house, but that was all I could do. I'm starving."

"Rei, see if there is any food left over from dinner which Jeremiah can have. If not, rouse the cook to make some food for our shivering visitor."

I was grateful for the care that was being lavished upon me by Azariah. It had been a long and difficult day in unusually unpleasant weather, and trying to find my way through the Chaldean army which encircled the city had left me feeling more like an old man than ever before. I had had no choice but to bring God's message to the king, but the effort required had taken its toll on me.

Azariah led me into the scroll room. He had obviously been working at his bench when the guard and I had interrupted him.

"What keeps the High Priest busy so late at night?" I asked.

"Affairs of state," he said loftily, then looked at me once more and added ruefully, "…and worry. I couldn't sleep. The Chaldeans attack the walls almost every day. New casualties and more damage every day." He held up a hand to quiet me as I leaned forward to speak. "And, yes, I know that you have been warning us for years."

There was a sound from the doorway and I turned to see my mother looking questioningly at me. The suspicion in her eyes turned to joy as she recognised me despite my dripping clothes and bedraggled appearance, and she ran to me and gave me a welcoming hug. Mothers often seem to know just the right thing to do to make their children happy, and that was exactly what I needed right then.

"Jeremiah!" she said. "I was wondering who this dripping and dishevelled desperado was – a man so eager to see the High Priest at such an hour. But son, you are very wet! And cold too. Are you hungry?"

"Yes, mother," I answered, "I am wet, cold and hungry. But Azariah has already started to do his best to fix all three."

"Excuse me," said Azariah, "I will just go and make sure that everything is progressing." He left the room and my mother and I were alone together.

"Why are you so wet and cold, Jeremiah?" my mother asked, looking concerned.

"I have been out in the rain and sleet, finding my way through the Chaldean army to get to the gate."

"I am glad that you have arrived safely, but why did you come? Jerusalem is full of fear and danger. Why would you come here? Jehoiakim is dead and King Jeconiah is desperately trying to find some way to escape the siege."

"King Jehoiakim is dead?" I asked, blankly.

"Yes, he was killed when the Chaldeans attacked," my mother responded. "Didn't you know?"

"No, I didn't," I mused, forgetting my discomfort in the light of this news. "But I suppose that things start to make a little more sense if that is true."

"What do you mean?"

"God told me to speak to the king and the queen mother.[2] That seemed a bit strange with Jehoiakim, since he has never listened to anything his mother Queen Zebidah said. But it makes much more sense with Jeconiah. In fact, unless he's changed, it's hard to say anything to him without saying it to his mother Nehushta as well. He always wants his mother beside him, and she's always giving him advice – normally bad." I wasn't the only one who thought that Coniah should grow up and stop hiding behind his mother's skirts.

At that moment, Azariah returned and told me that hot water and warm, dry clothes were waiting for me in the washing room.

I was eager to hear more details about the death of Jehoiakim, but the call of hot water and dry clothes was too strong.

"Hot water sounds like bliss. I can hear about Jehoiakim later."

---

[2] Jeremiah 13:18

"Be careful not to use too much water," warned Azariah. "Despite this rain, we still have to be careful not to use too much water. If we run out, that will be the end of the siege – and that will probably be the end of most of us, as you keep on reminding me."

Chapter 2

Beyond the gate

Part of Nebuchadnezzar's army had marched along the main road to Jerusalem, through the hill country, past Bethel, until they were approaching Jerusalem from the north. Once Jerusalem was in view, the mounted vanguard stopped and waited for the rest of the army to catch up as they prepared to encircle the city.

Jehoiakim had surrendered to Nebuchadnezzar, the new king of Babylon,[3] in his fourth year as king, shortly after the decisive battle of Carchemish, and had served him for the next three years. But then, in the seventh year of his reign, Jehoiakim had rebelled.[4] Tribute money no longer flowed in a golden river to Babylon, and orders from Babylon were ignored.

Four years later, it was the time for payback. Extending a large empire requires coordination, and rebellious provinces cannot always be punished

---

[3] Daniel 1:1; Jeremiah 25:1
[4] 2 Kings 24:1

immediately. Nebuchadnezzar had been busy extending and reinforcing his eastern and northern borders, but now his empire was growing nicely. Nebuchadnezzar was pleased that his renown was minimising the effort required to further extend the empire. In many cases, only a threat of action was required for nations to start negotiating for peace and loosening their purse-strings. Babylon was flourishing and Nebuchadnezzar's building programs in that glorious city were already becoming the stuff of legend.

But Judah and its king, Jehoiakim, were unfinished business.

Nebuchadnezzar's desire for universal respect and his ambition for a growing empire depended on punishing rebels severely. Smashing them, really.

The time had come.

Nebuchadnezzar was not with this division of his army: he was still busy elsewhere and would come shortly. He was with other troops as they moved down the coast of Israel, moving quickly to shut the door on Egypt, thus putting an end to their trouble-making – once and for all, he hoped.

Other detachments had also been sent to strategic places throughout Israel and Judah to plunder and pillage.

His orders to the army now approaching Jerusalem had been clear, and his commanders were experienced men.

The vanguard sat on their horses and waited. On the western slopes of Har Hatsophim, the Mount of Watchmen, they sat as watchmen. Their orders were to wait for the rest of the army, but they were always authorised to take immediate action if they believed it would bring great rewards. And so they watched, out of sight of much of the city and completely out of sight of those on the Mountain of Corruption and its little sister to the south.

On that afternoon, King Jehoiakim was to be found high on the little sister of the Mountain of Corruption. His father, Josiah, had cleared the hill of all idolatry and symbols of the multitude of gods who had been worshipped there by his father and grandfather, but King Jehoiakim had restored much of that infrastructure. His attendance on that particular day was to cost him dearly.

Autumn had merged into winter, with colder weather and frequent rain, but this was a bright, sunny afternoon, and when the king finished his worship, he descended to the Kidron and crossed it before blithely deciding to return to the city through the Benjamin Gate. Surrounded by his entourage, he rode up the cool valley before climbing its sides to join the main road which ran from Jerusalem to the cities of the north. Riding his favourite donkey, King Jehoiakim was enjoying the warmth of the afternoon as he turned onto the highway. He wasn't exactly drunk, but he wasn't completely sober either, thanks to the wine he had enjoyed while feasting with his closest friends and advisors in the late morning. To some extent it had been a celebration, as his advisors had finally all agreed that it was now too late in the year for Nebuchadnezzar to attack. The fighting calendar each year begins in early spring, so spring and summer were times of particular caution and worry. An invasion in early autumn was still possible, though, and King Jehoiakim had been quite concerned that Nebuchadnezzar might make his unwelcome presence felt as the weather cooled. But now his advisors had all agreed that the time for worry was over. Nebuchadnezzar would not come this year, they said, so King Jehoiakim could heave a sigh of relief, relax a little with his friends and thank his favourite gods.

On the night that I entered Jerusalem, I stood in front of the fire in Azariah's scroll room and he told me of the events in Jerusalem in recent weeks. I hadn't realised until that time just how close an eye Azariah kept on events in the palace, or how carefully he cultivated friendships among the king's friends and advisors.

The ice that seemed to fill my bones gradually melted in the warmth of the room as his story unfolded.

In the tale that follows, I have put together all of the information I learned on that first night with many extra details pieced together from the words of Ahikam, the son of Shaphan, and others in the subsequent weeks.

CR

Tempting delicacies filled the tables in Jehoiakim's room of feasting, and sweet wine loosened the royal tongue. When an advisor expressed his confidence that once again Baal, Asherah, and all the host of heaven had kept the nation safe from attack through another year, King Jehoiakim responded, "Yes, and they have even delivered us from that traitor Jeremiah with his never-ending doom and gloom."

Jehoiakim never did learn that his doom came from Yahweh, the one true God, not from me.

As Jehoiakim's donkey carried him up out of the valley of the Kidron, there was plenty of laughing and singing amongst his friends and advisors. No-one was paying much attention to things around them. Even the soldiers who went ahead and those who followed close behind were not as attentive as usual. The warm afternoon sunshine bathed them all in a golden light and the weight of worry had been lifted from their shoulders.

The army of Babylon was only a distant threat, and several months would pass before the threat must again be faced.

So they thought.

But in actual fact the army of Babylon was a very real and present threat, with the vanguard, probably several hundred mounted men, sitting quietly on their horses just to the north of the city, on the slopes of Har Hatsophim, waiting and watching. Though hidden from the watchers at the Benjamin Gate by a fold in the hillside, they were nonetheless visible to the watchmen above the Corner Gate at the western end of the northern wall of the city. Questions were being asked by those watchmen, and actions would surely follow eventually; but no-one knew just who the horsemen were, so no-one was quite sure what to do, or how urgent it was.

The watchmen to the west made cautious signals to their fellows above the Benjamin Gate, but the latter saw only the soldiers leading the king's richly dressed party out of the Kidron Valley and assumed that the signals referred to them. They acknowledged the signals, but did nothing else.

The commander of the Chaldean vanguard, seated on a powerful horse, was gazing towards the city, alert to any possible threat or opportunity. He saw the soldiers emerging from the Kidron Valley, with the king and his attendants close behind. By a quirk of topography, the Chaldeans could see the king's party on the side of the valley, but could not be seen by the guards at the Benjamin Gate.

If only King Jehoiakim or his attendants had looked to the north, now slightly behind them as they reached the edge of the valley, they would have seen the impending danger; but they were moving slowly, carelessly, almost languidly towards the highway. The guards atop the gate were watching as they ought, but the silent danger was hidden from their eyes.

At the Corner Gate to the west, the guards were still concerned, but they assumed that the jovial king's leisurely protectors and the relaxed watchmen at the Benjamin Gate were aware of the horsemen as they sat, ready to pounce. The king's party had climbed out of the valley and reached more level ground. For a brief time, they would be out of sight of the watching Chaldean vanguard as they made their way to the highway.

On the flank of Har Hatsophim, the man on the powerful horse raised his arm and kicked his horse into motion. Swiftly his men followed him and a river of horses began to flow downwards.

The thunderous pounding of hooves rolled across the ground as their pace quickened and they swept down the hillside onto the highway. Faster and faster, it seemed, they galloped towards the unsuspecting king and his party. The Chaldean commander on his galloping horse knew that his chances of success grew with every moment that passed without discovery. A successful strike now could save months of delays and thousands of Chaldean lives. Nebuchadnezzar would be pleased.

On the wall to the west, the watchmen knew suddenly, certainly, that something must be wrong. A trumpet sounded, and then another. Urgency made the trumpets stammer and scream. This was no calm practice, and the blemishes in the trumpeters' performance conveyed more than the calls themselves.

The soldiers with King Jehoiakim noticed the sounds from behind just as the trumpets blew from the wall. Confused by the unexpected storm of sound, they glanced toward the wall in doubt, then looked behind them with sudden terror.

Jehoiakim's guards erupted in a frenzy of action, while their king, his mind still befuddled with wine, looked around in worried surprise.

The Chaldean troop had just appeared over a fold in the ground, but though they were galloping with all the frantic speed they could muster, there was still time for the king and his party to reach the gates in safety if only calmness and speed could prevail.

At almost the same instant, the Chaldean horsemen came into the view of the watchers at the Benjamin Gate – a terrifying, thundering, threat. There was no time to think, no time to plan; just time to act. But what should be done? The gate must be closed against the attackers, but what of the king? He could not be locked out of his own city, left outside to fight against impossible odds.

The few soldiers at the Benjamin Gate were called from their confusion and led out through the gate by their captain. The gatekeepers made sure that they were ready to close the gates as quickly as possible, but they could not close them yet.

From the west, the trumpets continued their raucous warning, and a few horses began to emerge belatedly from under the archway of the Corner Gate. Their number was pitifully small, but maybe even a few would help to delay the thundering horde that threatened to overrun the royal party.

The squad of soldiers attending the king finally found their voices: "Your majesty," they shouted, "the gate! The gate! Hurry to the Benjamin Gate." Ozem, their leader, ran to the king and added, urgently, "As fast as you can, my lord. You will reach there safely, before those horsemen. But hurry!"

The king was shocked into action, if not into complete sobriety. Those of his advisors and attendants who were also on donkeys crowded forward, and together they began to hurry towards the gate, with the soldiers running alongside.

Donkeys are not as large as horses, but they can gallop almost as fast when adequately motivated, and the king's donkey was given great motivation by her rider. The running soldiers were quickly left behind as the donkeys scuttled away towards the gate.

King Jehoiakim was swaying badly as his mount galloped towards the city gate. Wine had slowed his reflexes and impaired his balance.

Down the highway galloped the Chaldean vanguard, although their pace had eased a little as the king's party seemed to be moving swiftly and easily towards the gate. But they hadn't given up completely, even though the surprise victory they had hoped for appeared to be slipping further from their grasp with every hurried stride of the king's donkey.

Then it happened. King Jehoiakim had swayed to his left and was leaning outward a little when the unbalanced load caused his donkey to stumble. A small misstep, a hurried change of gait from the donkey to regain her balance – these are the minute details through which God controls the future. But for King Jehoiakim, there was no future, except as mute testimony to God's power in foretelling and controlling the future.

A donkey's stumble, a king's desperate clutch at nothing, and the future changed before the watching eyes. Eleven years of evil reign came to an end in an instant as Jehoiakim slid from his saddle. A cloud of dust rose over him as he landed head-first, then bounced and rolled to a halt, no longer a person, but a shapeless bundle of clothes. The dust began to settle over the body. With her unbalanced load suddenly removed, the donkey galloped awkwardly on for a moment, stumbling and almost falling herself; then, as she found her balance, her gait smoothed and then she began to slow.

No-one ever looked very closely at the corpse; the cause of death was never determined.

Surely Jehoiakim's close friends and advisors stopped to give aid as they galloped to safety? But no, his friends and advisors were not the sort to selflessly sacrifice themselves. They hurried on.

The soldiers of his personal bodyguard, too, as they ran for the gate – surely they stopped to help their king? But Jehoiakim had been no friend to his soldiers. Even the looks cast over their shoulders as they ran were not towards their fallen king, but towards the terrifying, galloping, thundering rush of horses that seemed to leap towards them with renewed speed.

In the end, only the donkey stopped and trotted back to her master, possibly out of a sense of duty. She first nuzzled him gently and then nosed him more firmly, but there was no response.

Jehoiakim's party hurried through the gateway to safety without him, well ahead of the Chaldean horsemen. The scurrying soldiers coming along behind met the captain with his small force of soldiers as they ran from the Benjamin Gate towards the fallen figure of their king. Hurried shouting and wild gesticulation followed, before they all turned and sprinted back to the gate.

The few horsemen from the Corner Gate, who had been the first to leave the safety of the city walls in the face of the unexpected threat, were the last to seek safety there again.

They galloped over ground that was sometimes rough as they made for the road along which the king's party were still making their way into the city in self-seeking dribs and drabs. The dusty bundle of clothes that had been King Jehoiakim, with the donkey standing alone beside him, caught their eye, and they rushed to his side. As they neared the unmoving body, they swung their horses around to face the Benjamin Gate, ready, if possible, to collect the king and make for safety without delay. Two men began to swing hurriedly down from their saddles, but at that moment, Chaldean arrows began to fall around them. A horse screamed as an arrow struck deep, and his rider could do nothing to control the pain-crazed horse as it galloped off along the road towards the city. The other men quickly remounted and their horses rose to a gallop as they fled towards the Benjamin Gate, surrounded by a hail of arrows. Galloping with them was the king's donkey, urged along by a rider who had grasped her bridle in the moment while the group had stopped to check on the fallen king. In the confusion, even the king's donkey had warranted more attention than her master.

The last scene in the drama of King Jehoiakim's life was about to play out. The galloping Chaldean commander signalled to his men to stop and reined in his horse beside the body. It must have been clear to all that this body was that of an important man. Although the clothes were now dusty, they were made of expensive, brightly-coloured material, and the ostentatious jewellery still attached in various places and hung around an arm that protruded from under the cloak announced his significance in the world.

By this time most of the vanguard had come to a halt and were sitting on their horses, gathered around their leader. A few stragglers joined the rest at intervals.

A personal attendant had ridden slightly behind the Chaldean commander. Now a sharp command was heard and the attendant dismounted and walked over to the shapeless bundle of expensive clothes.

As he knelt down, there was a sudden movement on the wall and a flurry of arrows and stones began to fill the sunlit sky from the archers and slingers who now lined portions of the walls.

Methodically, the Chaldean horsemen lifted their shields over their heads, but it was clear that it was professionalism that caused the movement, not fear. Obviously, they believed that they were out of range. Sure enough, the arrows fell short, although some missed by only a small margin. However, the sling stones did not fall short. Unused to such weapons, the Chaldeans had misjudged their range, and soon stones were falling among the crowded mass of horses and their riders. Most did little damage, being deflected by shields or armour, but some struck home, and a few horsemen were driven back in their saddles, or fell heavily from their horses to the dusty road below.

The commander's response was immediate, signalling for most of the horsemen to retire beyond reach of the stones. About 50 horsemen remained, armed with bows themselves and eager to use them. Most of them trotted forward until they were within range, then quickly slipped off their horses, took aim and began loosing. Arrows filled the air in both directions, and the archers on the wall were abruptly forced to seek better cover themselves.

Still kneeling and bent over the body of Jehoiakim, the commander's attendant was looking for evidence of his identity. Occasional stones were still falling amongst the remaining horsemen who surrounded the body, but the Chaldean arrows were successfully disturbing the aim of the slingers on the wall, so there was little danger.

An arm of the corpse was lifted and those on the wall could see that the attendant was struggling with something, pulling at the hand. A few tugs and he must have got what he wanted, because he dropped the arm, then removed something from around Jehoiakim's neck. Standing once more, he took two objects to his leader: a signet ring, and a seal which had hung on a cord around the neck of the fallen king.

The commander took the ring and the cord and waved them derisively toward the watchers on the wall. A thicker cloud of arrows and stones was the only reply. Meanwhile, the attendant returned to the dead man, removing the jewellery and then trying to lift the body, intending to carry it to his horse so that this trophy could be displayed to the defenders when the time was right. But the body was heavy and awkward, and he struggled to lift it until another soldier came to help. Together, they lifted the corpse of the lifeless king and began to carry it towards a horse.

The body was being pushed onto the horse's back when the commander's attendant was struck in the arm by a stone. Shouting in pain, he let go and stepped back, and Jehoiakim's body collapsed once more to the ground. The commander acted swiftly and tied a rope to his saddle, then threw the other end of the rope to the uninjured man who had been lifting the body and barked out instructions. The rope was quickly knotted around Jehoiakim's body below his arms and the commander turned his horse and began to trot away. Soon the rope drew tight, and the body was dragged along the road, bouncing ignominiously.

Quickly, the remaining archers remounted and trotted away, taking their wounded with them. For a short distance, arrows continued to fall around them but they were soon out of range of all except sling stones.

Meanwhile the rope pulled Jehoiakim's body along the raised roadway behind the commander's trotting horse, sliding and rolling from side to side. Then a slight depression caused the body to twist and roll to the edge of the roadway and the rope caught beneath a large stone. A sudden jerk at his saddle forced the commander to stop, and urgent tugs failed to free the rope. With sling stones continuing to rain down around him, the commander abruptly pulled a knife from a scabbard on his belt and cut the rope. The unwanted body briefly settled with its legs hanging over the side of the road embankment, then slowly rolled off the roadway altogether.

King Jehoiakim's fall from prominence was complete.

Soon the Chaldean archers rejoined the rest of the vanguard beyond the range of even the best slingers and stopped to consider what they had found. The commander studied the signet ring and seal recovered from Jehoiakim, and the news of the identity of the corpse spread quickly through the company. Cheers rose and once again the commander waved the ring and cord above his head, jeering at the men who lined the wall.

Judah's king was dead – a mere bundle of clothes lying beside the king's highway, dragged and dumped beyond the gates of Jerusalem. When I heard these details, I felt no sympathy for this evil king; instead, my heart beat rapidly with excitement and awe.

Once again, the words of Yahweh had come true:

"With the burial of a donkey he shall be buried,
dragged and dumped
beyond the gates of Jerusalem."[5]

Within two hours, the rest of the Chaldean army had joined the vanguard and begun to spread out to encircle the city. Jerusalem was besieged.

℞

For three months and ten days, the body of Jehoiakim lay where it had been discarded, beyond the gates of Jerusalem. It lay in a no-man's-land between the city wall and a besieging army – an increasingly shapeless bundle

---

[5] Jeremiah 22:19

of once brightly-coloured clothing. He had once been a king, living in luxury and selfish idolatry. Now, he lay gradually rotting as the winter rains fell and refreshed the earth, until the days again began to lengthen.

No brave warriors risked their lives beyond the gate to retrieve the body. No-one sought to give their unlovely king a royal burial; in receiving the burial of a donkey, he got exactly what God had promised – and what he deserved.

Chapter 3

Inside Jerusalem

By the time I made my way into Jerusalem, Jeconiah had been ruling for almost three weeks.

The morning after my furtive entry dawned cool, but fine. The biting cold of the night before had passed, and stillness had replaced the furious gusts of rain, ice and sleet.

You might expect that a feeling of peace would follow, but instead, Jerusalem was a city filled with fear. The greatest army in the world was camped outside her walls, and everyone inside wondered daily whether this would be the day when an overwhelming, irresistible attack would be launched. No-one I spoke to had any confidence that the siege could be resisted successfully until the Chaldeans finally gave up and left. Instead, all felt fear and uncertainty about what would happen to them when the city fell.

No-one could enter or leave the city in an ordinary way, so those whose day-to-day work took them outside the city could no longer do that work. Of course, there was plenty of other work to do in the besieged city, but many of these people simply sat around sharing their worries and grumbling instead. The atmosphere was so pessimistic that many even of the inhabitants whose lives had not really been affected by the siege were stopping work and joining the malcontents. Already there were many items that could not easily be bought in the city, not because they were not available within the walls, but because the will to trade was lacking. One of the potters still working near the Potter's Gate was wondering why he bothered; as he said to me, "Why should I work hard to earn money that will all be taken from me by the Chaldeans – if they let me live at all?"

Most people had no hope and saw no purpose in fighting a war they could not win.

I couldn't help wondering whether God's prophecies had contributed to this pessimism. Had people actually believed the prophecies after all?

On that first calm morning, I made my way to the Benjamin Gate and looked out from the wall above the gate. Many of the king's guards were posted on the wall keeping watch over the Chaldean army.

"The Lord bless you, Jeremiah," called their captain, and I recognised him as one of the guards I had talked with from time to time at the king's palace. My work as a prophet has made me some interesting acquaintances over the years.

"The Lord keep you," I replied.

"Well, you were right about 'im, sir," he said respectfully, gesturing along the road below us. I must have looked a little unsure, because he added, "The ex-king, I mean." He spat contemptuously over the parapet and pointed to a place beside the road, some distance away, but nearer than the closest Chaldean camp fire that I had passed in the dark and rain a few hours before.

I looked where he pointed and saw what looked like a bundle of material lying beside the road – it must have been the body of Jehoiakim. The road between the wall and the nearest campfire was strewn with logs and boulders that had apparently been put in place by the Chaldeans to slow down any attacks from the city. Among these obstacles were more bodies, many lying in grotesque attitudes where they had evidently fallen and died in agony. I thought back to the obstacles that had made my progress so difficult in the pitch black of the previous night and suddenly wondered whether any of my stumbles had been due to tripping over one of these bodies. The idea was revolting from a practical point of view, but also deeply concerning: I was a priest, and contact with dead bodies caused uncleanness of a sort that I had always taken great care to avoid. Yet now I might inadvertently have made myself unclean by touching the body of friend or foe – or even of a king. I had not noticed any smell, but the stench of decaying flesh could easily have been hidden by the strong wind and rain. Was I unclean? The captain cleared his throat and brought me back from my musings with a start.

"You said the burial of a donkey, didn't you, sir?" he said. "It's funny, but his donkey was saved. She's happily munching straw in the royal stables, I'm told."

"God made the prediction, not me," I corrected him absently. "So yes, of course it was right."

"Ah, and what about the rest of us, sir? Will we die too, and join those other carcasses out there?" Once again, he gestured beyond the walls, and this time I looked more closely at the bodies that littered the road and its surrounds. Some wore Chaldean armour and clothing, yet lay with arrows protruding from their bodies where a chink in the armour had been found. Many round sling stones lay scattered on the ground, and several Chaldean helmets bore the marks of a heavy impact. Nearer to the gate, some of the bodies were clearly men of Judah, and most of these lacked armour and uniforms.

"Were all of those killed when the Chaldeans first attacked?"

"No, most of them were killed only yesterday. You see, a company of Chaldeans came down the road bringing a battering ram. It was a huge tree trunk hanging from chains on a long wooden trolley with large wheels, and they had a couple of companies of archers with them to give covering fire. There were about one hundred men pushing the trolley, while others went ahead to try to clear the road so that it could keep rolling. We started aiming for them from here, right where we are standing now."

The captain was completely engrossed in his story, giving me all the details of the Chaldean attack, and I must admit, I found it fascinating. He continued: "Archers and slingers, all of us trying to pick off the men clearing the road. You understand that if they couldn't clear the road, the battering ram couldn't come anywhere near the gate.

"That seemed to work well for a while, and the road was gradually being covered by dead and wounded men – and all of them Chaldean, which was even better. We were getting a few casualties up here, but we have the battlements to protect us, and it was much easier for us shooting down from on top than it was for them shooting up at us. And, quite frankly, slingers are better than archers in these situations anyway. They have a better range and people are always surprised by how much damage they can do. The worst part about them is that it's hard to sling a stone without completely exposing yourself to the enemy. We've had a few slingers hit just as they were about to launch their stones, particularly men who aren't really soldiers – the farmers and shepherds who came into the city for safety just in the last hour or so before the main units of the Chaldeans arrived. They are fighting alongside those of us who are in the king's standing army, but they're not used to trying to hide behind a shield while they use their sling. Lions and bears don't shoot arrows at you!

"Anyway, after a while, the Chaldeans brought up reinforcements, people carrying shields to protect the men as they cleared the road, and that made our job much harder. They also brought up more archers, and soon there was a hail of arrows all around us. A few men were even killed down in the market area behind us by arrows that flew over the wall. If you look down there…" he took my arm and turned me around towards the market area where I had stood and prophesied on several occasions over the years, "…you'll see that quite a few of the stalls still have arrows in their woodwork. And those burnt ones over there…" and he pointed to several stalls whose timber frames were charred and blackened, leaving only scorched remnants of the tent covers that covered most of the other stalls, "…a merchant in one of them was hit by an arrow and knocked over. As he fell, he knocked over a lamp, and that started the fire. It took a lot of work to get that fire under control, I can tell you, and more arrows kept falling in amongst them all the time."

I began to wish that I had been there to see the events he was describing in such a captivating way. I felt a little surprised, because I had always thought that in a siege, the attackers simply sat and waited for hunger or thirst to bring the defenders to their knees. This siege was obviously not working like that!

But my thoughts kept circling back to the fundamental reason for all this: God was bringing the punishment he had promised. How would it all end?

I shook my head to clear it of these morbid thoughts and asked, "So what happened with the battering ram? The gate doesn't look damaged."

"No," said the captain, "they didn't get to the gate. When they brought up more archers, they withdrew the men who had been trying to clear the road – took them back to where the battering ram was and formed them into a crowd of men surrounding the ram, with a roof of shields over their heads. That stopped the arrows getting to them, but the large sling stones seemed to be harder to stop. Some of our slingers began to send their stones right up high so that they came crashing down on them from the sky. The stones landed heavily on the shields and often broke through to hit the men underneath, particularly when they hit near the edges of the shields. So then they withdrew the men out of range of the slingers – probably trying to work out what to do next, but that was when we saw an opportunity. As you know, there is a small gate near the main gate below, leading out of the side of the main tower stonework. Normally we keep it barricaded up during a siege to make it harder for deserters who might make a quick dash for it, or for traitors who could quietly let in enemies in the dead of night, but we didn't want to open the main gate because it takes too long to close properly and that would be too risky. But a group of about thirty soldiers opened the small gate and filed out, then ran towards the battering ram carrying lighted torches and containers of oil and pitch. It took the Chaldeans a while to notice what was happening, and by that time the men had almost reached the ram. We stepped up the number of arrows we were shooting, and the sling stones as well.

"By the time the first of our men reached the ram, the Chaldean archers had worked out what was happening and were beginning to shoot at them. Some were hit, but others ran past the end of the ram nearest the gate, the end that was covered with metal to help with battering down the gate, and started pouring oil and spreading pitch all along that massive log. The flames spread quickly right along its length, but by then the Chaldeans who had withdrawn were running pell-mell back towards them.

"Some of our men had slings with them and there were enough stones around that those Chaldeans got a lot more than they counted on. Normally the stones can't get through armour directly, but they hit so hard that often they don't need to. And a lot of our slingers are amazingly accurate. I wouldn't have wanted to face them, I can tell you! For a while it was a glorious chaos: sling stones, arrows, spears and swords everywhere."

The captain's face was alight with the memory of battle, and a few of his men were standing around us, supporting his story-telling with grunts of agreement and fists raised in celebration. Other onlookers seemed less enthusiastic, and one of these said drily, "Yes, boss, and then what happened?"

The light left the captain's face and he looked deflated as he sighed and said heavily, "Then the Chaldean archers got their aim right and there were hundreds, no, thousands of arrows speeding towards our brave men. Within moments they had all been mowed down, and it was the Chaldean archers who were cheering. Their foot soldiers rushed to the battering ram and put out the fire, and that was the end of that." The men turned away slowly and looked down towards the road and the bodies which lay along and beside it.

"What happened after that?" I asked.

"Well, as you can imagine, we were all very angry and did the best we could to pay them back with arrows and stones, but anger doesn't always guarantee success. Angry slingers don't take as much care trying to hide, and I think we lost more men up here on the wall because of that. Then the Chaldeans took away their battering ram and we haven't seen it since. I suppose they will fix it up and bring it back again. Since then we have put more bars across the gate to strengthen it.

"They collected some of their dead, but by that time the weather was getting worse, with a strengthening wind – really cold it was – and rain starting too. As it got dark, we sneaked out and fetched some of our dead. We even found that one man was still alive, so we brought him in to patch him up, but the rest we had to leave." He waved his hand towards the sodden piles of material, and once again I wondered if I was unclean through contact with any dead bodies. I couldn't be sure, and it was unlikely that I would ever know, so I contented myself with looking down on the scene beyond the wall.

It was clear that wild animals had been picking at the bodies, and from time to time birds landed on the corpses and pecked at them. The sight made a big impression on me, although logic told me that nothing I saw should have been a surprise.

God had promised Jehoiakim an ignominious end, and so it had come to pass. Kings, even evil kings, were normally given a royal burial, but this king had received the burial of a donkey, discarded in a place where his body could be left to decay without causing too much trouble. Yet it had all come about in such a natural way: no angels needed to strike him down, no lightning from heaven to destroy him, just a vanguard's opportunistic manoeuvre, a hurrying donkey's stumble, a wine-slowed response, a fall, and a broken neck – all combining at the right time to bring to fulfilment the promised curse of Yahweh.

℈

Now that I was inside the city, I had to deliver the message God had spelled out to me. However, some of God's words for the king were still unclear to me. For instance:

"What will you say when they set as head over you

those whom you yourself have taught
to be friends to you?
Will not pangs take hold of you
like those of a woman in labour?"[6]

I had been told to speak to the king and to his mother, but I wasn't sure whether these words would refer to King Jeconiah or his mother or both. It is much easier to deliver Yahweh's words effectively if I can see what they might mean or how they could be fulfilled, so I tried to find out a little more about this new king first.

Jeconiah was young, only 18 years old,[7] and I couldn't help feeling amused at how young that appeared now that I was 46 years old, compared with how grown up I had felt after God had spoken to me at the tender age of seventeen. How our perspective on age changes as we get older!

His mother was Nehushta, the daughter of Elnathan of Jerusalem[8] and she was an evil woman. I was told that Josiah had had a hand in choosing her as a very young wife for his son Jehoiakim, and it seems that she may have initially leaned a little towards righteousness. But in the years since, she had shown some natural skills with evil, and had also proved to be a domineering mother.

In later years, King Jehoiakim and she had not got on well, but she had always treated him with just enough respect to ensure that she was not disposed of.

Jeconiah had two other names that he was known by: "Coniah", a more informal name used by his friends in a

---

[6] Jeremiah 13:21

[7] 2 Kings 24:8. Hebrew manuscripts of 2 Chronicles 36:9 say 8 years old, while Syriac and Arabic manuscripts of the verse say 18. The latter appears more likely, since the same verse states that he did evil in God's sight. Such a bad report is more likely for an 18-year-old than an 8-year-old.

[8] 2 Kings 24:8

friendly way or by his enemies in a dismissive way; and the most formal name "Jehoiachin", which was used in the writing of the national histories. Whenever God spoke to me about Jeconiah, he used the name "Coniah" or "Jeconiah", perhaps to emphasise the fact that a man's creator does not need to speak to him formally!

My enquiries revealed that Jeconiah was a real "mother's boy" who did what she told him most of the time. I also learned that there were exceptions to this, as is common with such men. He would often go out to find some freedom with his soldiers, not standing on ceremony with them, knowing that his mother would never come to look for him in such low company. Nehushta was a proud woman who would never even speak to soldiers or anyone so socially inferior to her. So Jeconiah was safe in their company, and enjoyed cultivating such people as friends and teachers.

I only began to see the possibility months later, but I think it was probably these friends that God was referring to when he spoke of friends being made head over the king or queen. Jeconiah had taken these soldiers as his friends, but he would not appreciate it when they became his supervisors a few months later. But more of that later.

Whilst making these inquiries, I was also trying to get an interview with the king. As a prophet who had spoken to the king's grandfather, and who was also the brother of the High Priest, I expected to be able to arrange to see the king without too much difficulty, and so it turned out. It was certainly easier than the first time I had tried to meet his father, Jehoiakim. On that occasion, Jehoiakim had deliberately made me wait to show his power over me.

Jeconiah agreed to see me the very next day, and as I was led into the throne room I thought back to the first time I had ever been in that room, led in by King Josiah himself after I had interrupted his destruction of an idol's altar and told him the words of God. I remembered how

Josiah had so thoughtfully and wisely negotiated with some incense-sellers, smoothing their ruffled feathers where possible, but also demanding a change to their behaviour where necessary. What a king Josiah had been! And how little remained of his work. How little his son, and now his grandson, had learned from his wisdom.

The throne still looked the same, but the young man who sat upon it looked much less confident than his father, and the chair which sat next to the throne was a new addition. Seated on this chair was a beautiful woman in her mid-thirties with striking red hair.[9] Her face showed a strength which was missing from the soft, fleshy face of her son, and at that moment, she looked anything but welcoming as I walked towards the dais.

I showed Jeconiah the respect due to a king, but it was hard to know how to treat the queen mother. She was wearing a finely worked golden crown inset with jewels, and the guards had advised me that she would expect acknowledgement, as was indeed shown very clearly by her expression. Her face was tilted up a little and she looked down on me from her place on the dais, then looked away from me towards her son. I had the feeling that she was trying to show him how he should be looking at me, and he seemed to be trying to imitate it. King of Judah he might be, but he was manifestly still subject to his mother! I decided to ignore her until God's message included her.

She cleared her throat, and Jeconiah took the hint. "Jeremiah, son of Hilkiah," he said, "you spoke many times to my grandfather, and often to my father as well. Now they are both dead, and I am king." He looked at his mother for guidance, but got none. He laughed a little awkwardly and continued, "My father used to say that

---

[9] The name "Nehushta" means "made of brass", which may refer to her hair colour.

your prophecies said much but gave little – that they demanded obedience from him, but offered nothing in return." Once again he looked to his mother for support, and this time she gave some.

"My husband said that you made many prophecies," she said, looking at me with a mirthless smile, "but that they never came true."

"Well, he couldn't say that any more, could he?" I responded, trying to speak gently, but wanting to make a point. I knew that there had been no apparent love between Queen Nehushta and King Jehoiakim, her husband, but it was possible that she was still upset by his death.

She looked a little puzzled, but certainly not upset. "Of course he can't," she said baldly, "he's dead."

"And in his death, God's prophecy was fulfilled."

"What do you mean?"

"Yahweh, the God of our fathers, predicted that he would be buried with the burial of a donkey. Dumped beyond the gates of Jerusalem. Kings are buried, but donkeys are not."

"Did you tell my husband this?"

"Yes, I did. It was a little more than a year ago. Had you not heard it?"

"No," she said shortly. "Where did you get this message from, anyway?"

"Normally God speaks to me as if there is a voice speaking all around me, but burning within me. And the words are written in my mind too, so that I can't forget them." It is always difficult to describe God's voice to others. I find it hard enough to choose words to describe it even within myself when I think about it. When considering it in my own mind, I often end up "thinking" the way it feels instead of trying to use words – but that doesn't work when I'm talking to others!

"So why do you think the words are from your God and not just your own imagination?" Nehushta asked, sarcastically.

"They come with a presence and a mind that is separate from me, and their mood and feeling are often quite different from how I am feeling at the time. Of course, one other reason I am sure the words are from God is that they speak of future things that come to pass. You see, God spoke more than once of King Jehoiakim's death and the events that have happened around it. Another time, he said:

"Therefore thus says the Lord
concerning Jehoiakim king of Judah:
He shall have none to sit on the throne of David,
and his dead body shall be cast out
to the heat by day and the frost by night.
And I will punish him and his offspring
and his servants for their iniquity.
I will bring upon them and upon
the inhabitants of Jerusalem
and upon the people of Judah
all the disaster that I have pronounced against them,
but they would not hear."[10]

"But what about me?" interrupted Jeconiah. "Here I am – sitting on David's throne. Your predictions have failed!"

"There is more to sitting on David's throne than just sitting on the fancy chair that his son King Solomon made. David ruled over all Israel. Even if we only consider the seven and a half years that he spent ruling over Judah, you still have not "sat on his throne" as he did.

---

[10] Jeremiah 36:30-31

You rule over Jerusalem. Who will obey your commands outside these walls? King Nebuchadnezzar of Babylon rules all of the rest of Judah. You do not sit on David's throne!"

King Jeconiah looked down at the floor for a few moments and then looked uncertainly at his mother. She responded by saying to me angrily, "What right has your God to inflict such a disgraceful death on my husband? He was the king of Judah: your king too! Why did you not show him the respect he deserved?"

I decided not to mention her own lack of respect for her husband, but pointed out instead that her husband had experienced the judgement of God, receiving exactly the respect he deserved.

Once again, Jeconiah interrupted to repeat the same question, "But what about me? I sit here on Solomon's throne. What will happen to me?"

"As with your father, to some extent that is up to you, but you haven't made a good start. Right now, God has a message for you, and that is what I came to deliver."

"But do we wish to hear it?" asked Nehushta, looking down on me disdainfully from her finely crafted and beautifully decorated chair. She turned away from me and looked at her son, her long red hair with its many jewels and braids swinging heavily around her shoulders as she did so. "O king, should we listen to the words he claims to bring from Yahweh?"

Jeconiah looked uncertain. I suspected that he was more used to being told what he thought than to being asked. After wavering for a few moments, he seemed to see a way to buy a short delay. He called to one of his servants, "Fetch Jeremiah a stool to sit on, while I decide what is best for the kingdom. Should we hear Jeremiah's words, or not?"

Chapter 4

The king and the queen mother

A servant brought me a stool and placed it on the floor near the dais, well below the king and his mother.

As I sat down, I watched Jeconiah and his mother, who were deep in quiet conversation. It seemed that they were genuinely unsure whether they should let me speak or not.

I sat quietly and waited for their decision, well aware that God's command for me to speak would override their decision anyway, but knowing that ignoring the king's command in his own throne room was a capital offence. The guards who stood around the room did not carry swords and spears for nothing.

It was quite a relief, therefore, when Jeconiah concluded his discussion by turning towards me and saying, "We have decided to let you speak, since you guarantee that these are the words of Yahweh."

"Thank you, my lord the king," I began. "About two years ago, Yahweh sent me to buy a new loincloth, telling me to wear it, but not to wash it. Then he told me to go and bury it near the Euphrates River. I did so. A few months ago, he instructed me to return to the Euphrates River and retrieve the loincloth. But when I dug it up, the cloth was ruined. No good for anything at all.

"While I was there, the word of the Lord came to me:

" 'Thus says the Lord:
Even so will I spoil the pride of Judah
and the great pride of Jerusalem.
This evil people, who refuse to hear my words,
who stubbornly follow their own heart
and have gone after other gods
to serve them and worship them,
shall be like this loincloth, which is good for nothing.
For as the loincloth clings to the waist of a man,
so I made the whole house of Israel
and the whole house of Judah cling to me,
declares the Lord,
that they might be for me a people, a name,
a praise, and a glory, but they would not listen.' "[11]

"A *loincloth*!" said Nehushta with distaste. "Doesn't God talk about Israel as his own special people? That sounds a bit more important than a *loincloth*, don't you think? You don't need a palace, a throne and a king with a jewelled crown to rule over a *loincloth*. I can tell you, Jeremiah, I wouldn't work so hard as queen mother if I thought of Judah as a dirty, rotting *loincloth*."

Jeconiah seemed to find her repeated references to loincloths more amusing than demeaning, but he diplomatically followed his mother's lead nevertheless. "Hasn't God spoken of Israel as his flock, and us kings as its shepherds?" he asked. "Isn't that what I am meant to be – a shepherd of God's people?"

---

[11] Jeremiah 13:8-11

"Yes," I replied, "you are. God told me:

" 'Say to the king and the queen mother:
"Take a lowly seat, for your beautiful crown
has come down from your head."
The cities of the Negeb are shut up,
with none to open them;
all Judah is taken into exile,
wholly taken into exile.
Lift up your eyes and see
those who come from the north.
Where is the flock that was given you,
your beautiful flock?' "[12]

"Yahweh didn't tell you those words, you made them up out of your head just then!" snapped Nehushta.

"No, you are wrong," I said gently. "They are God's words, delivered to me about two months ago. If they fit with what we were talking about, that is because God is God. And that is exactly why you should listen to his words of warning."

I looked seriously at Nehushta, but she looked away, so I looked at Jeconiah instead, who pursed his lips and stroked his thin beard. "It sounds too good a fit to be true. How can I know that you are telling the truth?"

Now I had a problem. As usual, I had written all of the words of God in a scroll shortly after I heard them, and I need only show Jeconiah the scroll to prove that the words had been written before today. That part was easy. But should I risk it? When Jeconiah's father had been shown a scroll with God's words, he had cut it up and burned it. Could I trust the son not to do what the father had done? I almost copied Jeconiah and stroked my own beard as I tried to make up my mind, but I managed to control the urge.

---

[12] Jeremiah 13:18-20

No, I decided, I would not offer this proof. Was not the death and non-burial of his father enough proof that I was telling the truth? Although the queen mother had not heard of them, the words had been proclaimed before the now-dead king in this very room, terrifying though the experience had been. Yet God had kept me safe even through that. Not only so, but the captain at the gate had known of them, and had referred to them the previous morning. The prophecy had not been forgotten.

"All the proof you need is in the prophecy about the death of Jehoiakim, your father," I replied firmly. "That prophecy is known throughout the city, and its fulfilment lies in plain view beyond the gate."

As I finished, there was a muffled thud from above and the whole room seemed to shake. Nehushta gasped and put her hand to her mouth. I looked around quickly and saw that, though the standing guards had looked up for a moment, they did not look as surprised as I felt.

"Another one," said Jeconiah, worriedly, before ordering one of the guards at the door, "Go and see if there is any damage." He turned back to me and said gruffly, "Jeremiah, that is all the time we can spare for you. The Chaldeans are attacking with their catapults again, and we must make plans to distract them."

There was no choice. I was escorted out of the palace and walked slowly down the steps, wrapped up in my own thoughts, wondering whether the king and his mother would listen to God's words at all. Suddenly, a guard at the gate shouted, "Look out!" and pointed towards the sky. I looked up just in time to see a large stone hurtling through the air before landing on the pavement in front of the palace. A cloud of dust rose and a shower of stone fragments filled the air. Fortunately for me, none of them came in my direction. The stone bounced and crashed into the wall that surrounded the palace, before ricocheting off at an angle and coming to rest near the guardhouse.

This was my first experience of the stones that the Chaldean army had been flinging into the city from their powerful machines, set up so swiftly and efficiently by the engineers who accompanied the army. Over the last week, the city had been terrorised by these stones, which made walking the streets of the city quite dangerous. Azariah had warned me about them, but we had not heard or seen any the day before – presumably the machines had been affected by the heavy rain. The mechanisms must now have dried out, and I had been given a firsthand demonstration of the frightening danger that they posed.

Glad to be uninjured myself, I looked back towards the guard who had shouted. He must have been directly in the way of the fragments generated by the stone striking the pavement, as one arm was bleeding and he was sitting on a bench near the gate with his hands to his head. Two other guards were already bending over him, trying to help. I walked over to see if there was anything I could do, but all I could do was talk to them. He was the only one who had been injured this time, and his helmet had protected him from the worst of the damage. A flying stone had struck his helmet with a heavy blow that had left his ears ringing, but he would be alright.

"How long are these stones going to keep coming?" one of the guards asked resentfully, as he tried to bind up his comrade's arm.

"Well, this is Judah," the other answered. "The hills around here aren't exactly short of stones, are they?"

"It's just a matter of time before we all get hurt or killed, or run out of food," said the injured guard.

"And what will the Chaldeans do to us then?" asked the first guard, as he finished tying up the bandage.

"Well, last time they killed lots of people," said the other, reminding us of the time when Nebuchadnezzar had briefly besieged Jerusalem seven years earlier, and then let his soldiers run wild in the city after Jehoiakim's surrender. "I'm certain it will be worse this time. They'll be making sure that we know what happens to nations who rebel against Nebuchadnezzar. It'll be a slaughter, a blood-bath. Particularly for us soldiers."

"Look out, here comes another one!" shouted the first guard, and we all spun around to look in the direction from which the last stone had come. Then we all dived for the ground. I felt completely unprotected, trying to hide in the open area in front of the palace, but fortunately this stone flew well over our heads, striking a building some distance from the palace with a deep, reverberating thud.

In the past, we could have returned their fire with the same sorts of machines. In fact, when King Uzziah had reigned 150 years before, Jerusalem had been well equipped to defend herself, attacking any besieging army with large stones and arrows fired from similar machines.[13] But vassal kingdoms are not allowed to maintain powerful weapons like that, and over the years Uzziah's machines had all been destroyed. Even after Jehoiakim had rebelled against Nebuchadnezzar, the tribute money saved had not been directed into defence. Sadly, Jehoiakim had never been given very much good advice – not that he had ever listened to good advice anyway.

So the Chaldeans could sit outside our walls and lob rocks at us with no fear of us replying in kind. They were cautious about our archers and slingers, but the siege walls they had built in many locations around the city provided good protection against these.

----

[13] 2 Chronicles 26:14-15

Unable to do anything to help, I left the palace and returned to the High Priest's house. More stones flew overhead, but none came close enough to cause me any concern.

In fact, my main concern at that moment was ritual cleanness. I wanted to re-read God's instructions about dead bodies and uncleanness. I had relived my stumbling, tripping walk along the road to the Benjamin Gate in the rain and windswept darkness many times, and had even tried to match my missteps to the locations of the bodies that still littered the road. Had I touched any of them? There were so many that I began to wonder: was it really possible that I had missed them all?

Azariah had copies of many scrolls, and eventually I found the scroll in which the wilderness travels and censuses of the people of Israel were described. I was sure that it contained the information I was looking for about uncleanness due to dead bodies.

Before opening the scroll, I explained my quandary to Azariah and my mother. They agreed that there didn't seem to be any easy answer, but that it might be easiest to assume I was unclean. Naturally, though, that raised the question of whether I had made others unclean through my touch. Where did the results of such an accidental sin end? Had I made the High Priest unclean and spread that uncleanness to the very temple of God? At that point, I stopped speculating. It was best to read God's word first before getting too deeply entangled in the possibilities.

> "Whoever in the open field touches someone who was killed with a sword or who died naturally, or touches a human bone or a grave, shall be unclean seven days."[14]

---

[14] Numbers 19:16

This instruction was followed by a description of how the unclean person must be sprinkled with the water for impurity[15] on the third and seventh days. After washing his clothes and bathing his body on the seventh day, the unclean person would finally be clean again.[16]

They were clear and simple directives, and they matched my memory. I had learned these rules from God's scrolls at the time, now so long ago, when there had been a revival of our knowledge of the law of Yahweh – after the eighteenth year of King Josiah. These were the rules that we priests were meant to know as second nature, and teach to the people as well. But none of them included a situation like mine where the touching of a dead body might have happened, but one could not be sure.

This was the sort of situation that my brother revelled in: an analytical assessment of the known laws and their application to cases that were not quite so simple. But this one was closer to home than he liked. In his ordinary assessment of such a case, historical precedent would have argued that if there was uncertainty, it was best to assume the worst. But if we assumed the worst in this case, that meant we had to take these words to heart too:

> "And whatever the unclean person touches shall be unclean, and anyone who touches it shall be unclean until evening."[17]

Assuming the worst would mean that I was unclean and that everyone and everything I had touched since I entered the city was also unclean. Not only that, but if the word "it" referred to anything or anyone I touched,

---

[15] Made by mixing water with the ashes of a red heifer (see Numbers 19:7) which was offered from time to time as described in Numbers 19:2-10.

[16] Numbers 19:17-19

[17] Numbers 19:22

then anyone who had touched people or things I had touched would also be unclean.

Azariah, my mother, many of the guards at the gate and some of the guards at the king's palace: all of them would have been made unclean through my touch. Not just that, but anything that they had touched or that had touched them would also be unclean until evening.

Uncleanness was certainly catching!

What was the best answer? It all depended on whether I had touched a dead body or not, and I simply didn't know.

What would God want? What was his intention in these instructions? Clearly, God wanted us to remain clean, and his instructions about priests allowed us to deliberately become unclean only for our nearest relatives if they died.

Then reality struck as I saw the greater problem: did I ever know if I was really clean? I thought of the multitude of ways in which people could become unclean and then pass that uncleanness on to me without my knowledge. Was I ever truly clean while among my people?

A similar problem had concerned me before when visiting other nations as a prophet, and I had concluded then that all I could do was to do the best I could to avoid any uncleanness that would arise from my own actions. The actions of others – those who did not try to follow God's laws of cleanliness – I had decided to ignore unless they told me themselves of things that would make me unclean. I kept my eyes open and was cautious, but if I was ignorant of something, all I could do was to ignore it and pray that God would forgive and cleanse me.

I have spoken at length about my mental struggles at this time, and you may feel that I was being foolish, but I had to explain how a proper obedience to God's law depends on the whole nation keeping his law. An individual cannot really keep himself holy in an unholy nation without completely leaving society. God had sent me to be a prophet to the nations, and becoming unclean without knowing it was an inevitable hazard for me. Now I had seen clearly that the same was true even among my own people. No wonder God spoke of his nation as unclean!

Finally, I decided not to assume that I was unclean. If my nation had been striving for holiness, I would probably have decided otherwise, but when my entire nation was unclean and happy to have it so, it seemed foolish to concentrate on the ritual cleansing of an uncleanness that I had no reason to believe had actually occurred! Turning the nation back to God was the only way to cure uncleanness in Judah, but even Josiah had failed in that.

My brother agreed with my conclusion – which surprised me at the time. We only ever talked about my reasons, never his, and as he too is dead now, it is too late to discuss his motivation. But thinking about it later, I made my own guesses as to why he came to this conclusion, though of course I can't be sure. If I had pronounced myself unclean, Azariah would have had to do the same, and that would have been quite a shameful thing. It would probably have been the first time for centuries that a high priest had declared himself unclean because of a dead body. History has left our records incomplete, but the last time that we know of such a thing happening was in the time of king Joash, when events occurred that no-one in either the temple or the palace wants to talk about.

℆

Two days later, the Chaldeans attacked again with the battering ram – but by this time the ram had been coated all over with metal plates. On this occasion, there had been more careful preparation, and a larger force of soldiers accompanied the ram. No careless withdrawal of troops left the ram unprotected even for an instant, and the covering fire of archers made the top of the wall a very dangerous place to be. Thousands of arrows missed their targets on the walls and fell in the temple area or in residential areas well beyond. Some bounced harmlessly off pavements or stone walls, while others terrified or injured the inhabitants.

Outside the walls, a desperate battle was developing. The Chaldean units attacked with speed and precision, but from a vulnerable position. Archers and slingers all along the northern wall of the city could target the infantrymen who cleared the road ahead of the heavy wheels of the massive ram. Chaldeans with large shields did their best to protect the infantrymen, but such shields are heavy and slow to move. Arrows fired from further along the wall could outflank the shield-bearers, and many of the attackers fell wounded.

Once again, the attackers were forced to halt, but this time there was no opportunity for an attack from within the city. Extra Chaldean archers came swiftly forward to engage the archers and slingers on the wall, drawing their fire. The large Chaldean catapults had been re-targeted, and large rocks began to fall near both the Benjamin Gate and the Corner Gate. Some struck the top of the wall, falling among the crowded defenders, sending rock splinters flying and injuring many. Some men were even struck directly by stones and killed instantly.

The battle was not going well for those who defended Jerusalem, but they still held a commanding position of power. If they could only keep the battering ram away from the gates, the Chaldean army would not be able to quickly force an entrance to the city. Yet even the gates were formidable defences. Massive wooden planks and bars formed a protection that even a Chaldean battering ram would struggle to beat down.

Gradually more and more Chaldean troops were committed to the combat, but still the ram was unable to approach the gate. Casualties were high on both sides, but particularly amongst Nebuchadnezzar's men, and after several hours of determined but unsuccessful assault, the commanders gave the order to withdraw.

Inside the city, there was damage to be mended and casualties to be tended to or buried. News was taken to the king and the queen mother as they mulled over events and options with their advisors.

The city could not continue to bear the accumulating cost in manpower and infrastructure. Tactics must change – but what was the best way to resist? They knew that the surrounding army – already proving so hard to resist – was just the first hint of Nebuchadnezzar's power.

We later found that Nebuchadnezzar had directed his forces to press the siege aggressively in the hope of overcoming resistance within days or weeks, but casualties were mounting, and the commanders were reaching the stage where their approach must be reconsidered and scaled down.

Often patience can win where aggression fails.

Hunger can weaken when arrows cannot overwhelm.

A city can be starved into submission.

For empire builders, a prolonged siege is expensive: practically, it ties up troops; psychologically, it reduces an empire's authority. A lightning-fast defeat of uncooperative kingdoms spreads terror among nations. Existing vassal states are more likely to pay tribute; newly targeted nations are more likely to give in without a fight when faced with a demand for tribute. This was Nebuchadnezzar's ideal. His goal was an empire built of gold – the gold of vanquished foes.

Chapter 5

When and what?

I found living in a city under siege a novel experience, but not a pleasant one. Walking around the city was dangerous because of the many stones flung by the Chaldean catapults and the arrows that frequently overshot the walls when their infantry attacked. I was sure that it was just a matter of time before the Chaldeans conquered the city.

I need to explain once again that, even as a prophet, I did not know quite what was going to happen. The final result of this siege was to prove as much of a surprise to me as to anyone else – possibly more so. God had told me of destruction and desolation, of terror on every side, and had etched the words of the prophecies in my mind so that I could not forget them. But there is a big difference between knowing and understanding. God always fulfils his prophecies – except when he doesn't because people change. Nineveh has always stood out in my mind as a beautiful example of this. For Nineveh, the 40 days which were to usher in destruction came and went without the promised destruction falling on them because their repentance had changed the scene. Jonah's prophecy did not *fail*, it was superseded.[18]

Could God's prophecies of destruction through me be superseded? I did not know, but I did know that without some positive, earth-shaking change, every word that God had spoken through me would come to pass.

That part was easy to understand. However, I have always been caught by not being able to understand God's timing.

Time after time, I have expected his words to be fulfilled soon – with no more delay! – but time after time I have had to wait.

Time after time, I have delivered his words of imminent destruction, only to later receive further words that offered yet another chance of repentance.

At that particular time, almost 30 years of my life had been spent prophesying a destruction that was still "just around the corner", instead of actually happening! I don't like to admit it, but it was frustrating, and my frustration grew a little with each passing year. I was frustrated because God was not doing things my way.

Yet God had never said that he would do things my way. Instead, I had agreed to do things his way, and now I was baulking at that commitment. Seeing things God's way with God's timing is still completely beyond me. All I have learned to do (mostly) is to accept that I must wait patiently.

When would God fulfil his prophecies about Jeconiah?

---

[18] Jonah 3:4-10

Azariah had invited me to stay in his house, and I decided that it was probably best to do so. There were various others I knew in the city who would have been willing to host me, and I'm sure that I would have felt more at home with them, but it seemed rude to leave my brother's home when he was willing for me to stay. It seemed likely that conflict would arise – somehow, it always did between us – but I would have to sort that out when it came.

The High Priest's house was large, and only Azariah and his wife Hephzibah normally lived there, as both of their children had married and moved into homes of their own. Hephzibah could speak of little besides her children and grandchildren, and this reminder of the inexorable marching of the years made me feel briefly as if life had passed me by. While I had neither wife nor family, Azariah's oldest son, Seraiah, was now 27 years old – almost old enough to become a priest. He had married early, and his son Jehozadak was already seven years old. The line of high priests could continue if God wanted it to. But would any of them actually listen to Yahweh, the God they were meant to represent?

As for my line, it would finish with me. That was not my choice, but God's.[19]

ᑳᗉ

The task that had brought me into Jerusalem was completed, so what was I to do? Despite urging from friends and enemies alike, I was not willing to join those fighting the attacking Chaldeans. Although some prophets have joined Israel's army in the past, it seemed absurd that I should publicly announce that God's judgement was coming at the hand of the Chaldeans and then fight against them!

---

[19] See Volume 2 – As Good As It Gets, Chapter 16.

Some people in the city were working hard, but these were mostly the men involved either in its defence or in providing equipment for the defenders. Metalworkers were busy making swords and armour plates, leatherworkers were making protective clothing for archers and slingers, and fletchers were busy making new arrows or repairing Chaldean arrows that had been damaged when they landed inside the walls. Many others were doing nothing at all, and I did not want to be like them.

But what should I do? I had no pressing commitments: God had given me no new messages to deliver, and Azariah had made it clear that I was not needed as a priest. Since no-one could enter or leave the city, there was even less demand than usual for priests. I decided to take the opportunity to spend time with friends – the few I had left – and also within the temple.

Azariah had told me that our brother Gemariah was in the city, so I quickly took the opportunity to visit him. Gemariah had worked hard in his career as a priest, but that work had finished when he had turned 50 in the eighth year of Jehoiakim. Since then he had worked in an administrative role, directing the Levites who helped the priests with many of the tasks around the temple. He and his wife Abigail had no living children after the sad deaths of their two infant sons Hasshub and Hananiah. They had avoided giving in to bitterness completely, but they were not a happy couple.

Gemariah spoke of the ongoing siege and expressed confidence that neither the city nor the temple would be badly damaged. I was so convinced that the destruction of Jerusalem was near at hand that I nearly let myself off the very tight leash on which I have learned to keep myself, but something held me back. It was wise, and later I felt that the guidance had come from God.

It's hard to describe how I felt – I was so sure that my interpretation of God's prophecies was correct that I didn't even think of it as "interpretation" – just the obvious meaning. Clear and simple. But events were to show that I was wrong. If I had let myself speak freely, I would have been strongly advocating an understanding of God's prophecy that later proved to be wrong. In my opinion, this is one of the most serious ways in which I can fail as a prophet, and yet it is so easy to do. To properly represent God to others, I need to know and understand him, and who is equal to that task? So I have tried to learn to speak God's words loudly and often, but to say very few of my own.

Naturally, this is one of the concerns I have with writing this diary: as you read it, please remember that my words and thoughts cannot be trusted like God's words can.

❧

Jeconiah had been anointed king to replace his father, and his mother had taken the position of chief advisor without asking anyone. Together, they had sought advice regarding the defence of the city and the administration of the realm. In their quest for advisors, the name of Ahikam, the son of Shaphan, had come up. The fact that he had rarely been consulted during the reign of Jehoiakim actually worked in his favour, because both Jeconiah and Nehushta were seeking a new path, eager to step away from Jehoiakim's self-serving parade. Yet, in truth, their attitudes were little different from those of the king they replaced, and their desire for a different appearance held no promise of any meaningful change. Jeconiah's goal was to have his name written in history as a turning point in the kingdom of Judah, a signature of regeneration.

How grandiose our dreams can be.

Ahikam knew the quality of the man and exactly who was boss in the kingdom, but the desire to be involved once more in the inner circle of power proved too strong to resist. Eleven years in the wilderness of obscurity during the reign of Jehoiakim had been too long for a clever and ambitious man like Ahikam. Though he had not lost his influence completely, he had had little contact with the king and had never been invited into the inner group of trusted advisors. He had missed the awe of the populace, the immediate respect that the king's top advisors could demand. In occasional unguarded moments over the years, he had admitted to me his yearning for public adulation, while also acknowledging that his banishment from Jehoiakim's inner circle was a blessing, in that it separated him from the company of a king for whom he had very little respect.

But now, the moment beckoned, and he could see an opportunity to make a genuine contribution to the kingdom.

His family and mine had been quite close in our fathers' times and earlier, and Ahikam and I had become friends, despite our different outlooks on life. I found his analytical approach to administration fascinating. He had opened my mind to understand how a kingdom works in many areas.

His insights had also helped me to see how hard it was for a king to pursue ideals when so many experts promoted "practicalities" instead. There were always more who wanted to question and criticise than to support.

It proved to be just as hard for him as an advisor. Poor Ahikam. He was being offered a delicacy, an irresistible confection, a tasty morsel that would tempt him too much – the opportunity to wield influence and guide the hand of power; but not the power that really matters.

"King Jeconiah has been considering his options in the siege," he told me one afternoon when we met at the gate of temple. Ahikam was no stranger to the temple, and his commitment to Yahweh as our God always seemed genuine. But… and I'm afraid I can't really finish the sentence. His commitment was different from mine. For him, God was close, but not too close. Closeness to God has pros and cons, and many a man has striven to keep him at arm's length. But it never seems to work. As I have mused on this over the years, I have become more and more certain that through life we either keep getting closer to God or grow more distant from him, often without even realising it.

If I had any sons to give advice to, it would be to never try to control God. It sounds ridiculous for the clay to imagine it could ever control the potter, but I feel the temptation to try every day. I also sense that this single idea has contributed more than any other to my friends and family fighting against the messages God has given. I have read in the writings about the judges of Israel that in those days each man did what was right in his own eyes, and that is just what I mean.

"I suppose there are some choices," I said cautiously, "but surely not many?"

"Of course, I can't discuss all of the possibilities in detail," he responded, in the manner of one who feels some sympathy for a friend who is unable to share in his position of importance, "but the available choices have the ability to make a profound difference to the future of our nation."

"But what if there is no future for our nation? At least, not as a kingdom?"

"Of course there is a future. God made promises to Abraham. They can't fail. Judah will continue. Yahweh made promises to David about his sons reigning forever." He smiled and placed his hand reassuringly on my arm. "You have pointed these things out to me yourself, Jeremiah."

"True," I answered, "but God's promises to David's sons were conditional. If they obeyed God, they would continue to sit on the throne in Jerusalem. But ask yourself, have they obeyed?"

"Not completely of course, but God forgives."

"If there is repentance, yes," I agreed. "Can you use your influence to encourage Jeconiah to repent? To reform the kingdom? He seems to respect his grandfather more than he ever respected his father."

"Are you trying to get me sacked?" Ahikam laughed, but there was a note of seriousness in his voice as he continued, "At the moment I can't do anything like that. Maybe in a while – after this crisis is over. But for now, we need Jeconiah as king, and he needs us to support him."

"What about his mother, then? She's the one who really wears the signet ring."

"Of course, I can't really agree with you in that," said Ahikam cautiously, shaking his head slowly while looking around to see if anyone was listening. It was obvious that his spoken disagreement reflected a sense of duty more than any real conviction.

When our conversation finished that afternoon, we parted, Ahikam leaving the temple to speak again with the king of Jerusalem, and I entering the temple to speak with the king of all creation. If only we could have continued our discussions and I could have done a better job of convincing him that it was Yahweh we needed, not

Jeconiah. Ahikam was a good friend, but his interests and ambitions were leading him towards disaster.

CR

"A loincloth? You talked to Nehushta about a loincloth?" Zaccai laughed heartily and looked sideways at Abigail his wife, who smiled back at him. Apparently, she had known Nehushta before the latter became Jehoiakim's queen.

We were sharing a meal in their house and I had mentioned God's mission that had sent me twice to the Euphrates River and then required me to try to explain the lesson to King Jeconiah and his mother.

"Yes," I confirmed. "The king seemed to find it funny."

"And what about Nehushta?" smiled Zaccai. "I wouldn't think she would find it funny. A little beneath her, I would expect."

"You're right," I agreed. "She was all hoity-toity about it, but neither of them listened to the lesson anyway."

"I'm not surprised," said Zaccai. "But I hear that Ahikam is being taken back into the inner circle, so maybe they will start to hear some better advice."

"Has Jeconiah ever asked for your advice at all?"

"We have spoken a few times, but I don't think the queen mother likes me, since I'm one of his relatives, and was one of King Josiah's advisors in the good old days. Maybe he would listen more to Daniel if he were here – Daniel always had an amazing way with words, and he seems to keep on getting better."

Zaccai and Abigail's son Daniel had been taken into captivity in the fourth year of Jehoiakim along with many others, but his parents still heard news of him from time to time. When I had last heard, he sounded to have an even harder job in Babylon than I had here in Jerusalem, but he seemed to be handling it astonishingly well. A brilliant young man, but so determinedly righteous as well.

"Have you heard more news of him?" I asked.

"Yes, just a few months ago," said Zaccai, and his eyes glowed with pride as he looked across at Abigail and they smiled at each other. "He is constantly in Nebuchadnezzar's palace because of his integrity and wisdom. But the story we heard from him most recently was about his close friends, Hananiah, Mishael and Azariah – leaders in the province of Babylon they are. Apparently King Nebuchadnezzar set up a large golden statue on an enormous pedestal and ordered everybody to bow down to it. Those three refused to bow down to his statue and stayed standing while everybody else around them bowed down. The king was furious, but he still gave them an opportunity to recant: told them that all would be well with no questions asked if they obeyed. But would you believe it? They refused! Stood right in front of the king and told him that they couldn't do it. Just like that. Straight to his face. Well, the king was furious enough before, but after that response he was utterly apoplectic. He had them thrown into a fiery furnace."[20]

"Oh, that's terrible," I said, frowning, upset to hear of the deaths of such faithful men.

"Ah, that's where you're wrong," replied Zaccai with a wide smile. "They didn't die. Daniel wrote that the king looked into the furnace and saw four people in there, not just the three he had ordered burned – and all walking around. I suppose he must have felt a bit silly doing so, but he called to them in the furnace, very politely, and asked them to come out."

---

[20] Daniel 3

"How many came out?" I laughed, pleasantly intrigued.

"Only three," said Zaccai.

"But they were all perfectly alright, and their clothes didn't even smell of fire," said Abigail earnestly.

"Then the king announced that no-one was allowed to speak against Yahweh their God on pain of death," Zaccai concluded with a look of triumph.

"Amazing," I said, excited by such a rousing story of faith.

"Yes," agreed Zaccai, "and surely King Nebuchadnezzar won't treat us too badly when this siege ends if he is saying things like that. Maybe he will even lift the siege," he finished, hopefully.

"Don't forget that he is just God's servant – his tool, really," I argued. "God foretold destruction for Judah well before Nebuchadnezzar was king. Nebuchadnezzar will do what God ordains."

"We tell you a happy story of faith and victory," replied Zaccai reprovingly, "and you want to drag us all down into depression again! Can't you be happy and hopeful for once?"

"God will choose what happens in the end, but destruction is what he has promised so far. If we don't repent, the condemnation won't change."

"It's not really that bad, Jeremiah," said Zaccai and, sadly, I feel that he really believed it.

Despite the idolatry that still filled the city, the false prophets who choked the air with lies and the widespread immorality that flourished with no condemnation from king, prophet or priest; despite all of these signs that a flood-like judgement was warranted, he truly believed that our nation was "not really that bad".

Tragically, events have shown that I was right: there was no reason for optimism.

Would events have followed a happier course if Daniel and his three friends had remained in Jerusalem? Could they have sparked the reformation we needed? Could anyone?

☙

As that cold and rainy winter progressed, I spoke to many other uncles, cousins, nephews and friends. A growing fear for the future pervaded these conversations, but no-one wanted to start a grass-roots movement pushing for national repentance. No-one wanted to look to Yahweh our God for any answers – not even my brother, the High Priest.

Early in the winter, some urged the development of large catapults to match the Chaldeans' weapons, but as time passed, more and more suggested surrender, hoping thereby to minimise the bloodshed and loss. Nevertheless, a widespread fear of how much blood the Chaldeans might shed if they were allowed into the city meant that hanging on and hoping was still the most popular option.

As spring drew closer, Yahweh's words from the past burned more fiercely inside me, driving me to deliver and keep delivering his admonitions and commands around the city to an unwilling audience. Each day I spoke of terror and destruction, and my audience responded politely or rudely as they chose. On the next day, I would repeat the charade with a different audience. But none of the words made it through their armour, and after a month of this, it was clear that their patience was wearing thin. Not even fear could soften their stubborn hearts.

There were just a few who were less stubborn.

One such man was Meshullam, a Levite whom I had come to know and admire in the days of Josiah,[21] and who was now very old. He had helped to supervise the restoration of the temple in Josiah's reformation, and still spent a lot of time there. Although Levites had to retire from assigned tasks in the temple at the age of 50, they could still help with the work if they wanted to.[22] In a society that did not take God seriously, few tithes were received, and any income that there was went to those high in the priestly hierarchy. So most of the retired priests and Levites had no interest in helping with work in the temple, but instead took the opportunity to ensure an income in their old age. All too often this involved taking bribes or blackmailing people. But Meshullam was an exception. His work as a Validator when Josiah had ordered copies to be made of the Book of the Law had sparked within him a great love for reading the word of God. He tried to keep aloof from the godless lifestyle that pervaded both the city and the temple, but it was a difficult task. When he could, he helped with work around the temple, and his knowledge of the law helped some to remain closer to it than they would have otherwise. His particular love was for music and the Psalms with their unending admiration for Yahweh.

At that time, he had a young friend, Ezekiel the son of Buzi.[23] Buzi was a priest who was just a few years older than me, and Ezekiel was his youngest son, then in his mid-twenties. Ezekiel was showing himself to be very devout. Although he was not yet old enough to be ordained as a priest, he was doing his best to learn holiness from God's law. Meshullam had taken over his training and they were frequently seen together, mulling over the meaning of the words of the law, the Psalms or the

---

[21] See Volume 2 – As Good As It Gets, Chapters 11 and 12.

[22] Numbers 8:26 (the meaning of this verse varies between translations).

[23] Ezekiel 1:1-3

prophets – apparently Ezekiel was particularly interested in prophecies of the future. It was this that brought me into contact with him. Meshullam knew my attachment to the prophecy of Isaiah, gained through the "smelly scroll" that I had read countless times since I had first come across it in our scroll room back home in Anathoth.[24] As scrolls of scripture had become more readily available during Josiah's reign, my father had given me the scroll to keep. It had then travelled extensively with me through the many countries to which God had sent me as a prophet to the nations.

One day, Meshullam asked me to join them in looking at a passage in Isaiah's prophecy where the incomparable greatness of God is described and contrasted with the foolishness of idolatry.[25] We discussed it and lamented the many small symbols of idolatry that had slowly spread during the reign of Jehoiakim and now filled all corners of Jerusalem, and even of the temple. All three of us would have dearly loved to remove them from God's city as Josiah had done years before, but what could we do? We all felt powerless. I wonder how much more we should have done.

"Listen," said Meshullam:

> " 'Even youths shall faint and be weary,
> and young men shall fall exhausted;
> but they who wait for the Lord
> shall renew their strength;
> they shall mount up with wings like eagles;
> they shall run and not be weary;
> they shall walk and not faint.'[26]

"Now, Jeremiah, are these words general in nature or are they a prophecy of a particular time?"

---

[24] See Volume 1 – Early Days, Chapters 11 and 12.

[25] Isaiah 40:9-31

[26] Isaiah 40:30-31

"I believe that they speak of a specific time. If it was just a general statement for all time it would say, 'Even youths faint and get weary', but that extra 'shall' suggests that it speaks of a certain time or event when even youths will faint and get weary. I think it is probably still in the future."

"Are the 'wings like eagles' literal?" pondered Ezekiel.

Meshullam responded, "God said to our fathers in the wilderness, 'You have seen what I did to the Egyptians, and how I bore you on eagles' wings and brought you to myself.'[27] That wasn't literal."

"No," I agreed, "and I don't think it is likely to be literal here either. It seems to be just a picture of what 'renewing their strength' will be like for people who trust Yahweh and want to be near him."

"But there are beings with wings around God, aren't there?" asked Ezekiel eagerly.

"Well, yes, Isaiah spoke of seeing seraphim with *six* wings![28] One of the seraphs touched Isaiah's lips with a burning coal to burn away his guilt."[29]

"Oh, what a wonderful thing to see," breathed Ezekiel, his eyes wide with awe. "Have you ever seen anything like that, Jeremiah?"

I told him what I could of my encounters with God and the visions he had given me since that first night back on my seventeenth birthday. When I finished, he said in a breathless voice and with a look of yearning in his eyes, "How I long to be close enough to God to see such wonderful things!"

Here was another young man who loved God just like Daniel and his three friends did, and of much the same

---

27 Exodus 19:4

28 Isaiah 6:2

29 Isaiah 6:6-7

age as well. Maybe these young men were a direct result of the work of Josiah. If only he had lived to see their godliness.

Chapter 6

Surrender?

Time passed and the days began to lengthen again. Still the Chaldean army camped around the walls of Jerusalem. Each day, stones from their catapults caused more damage, injury and death. Each day, the morale of the ordinary people in the city seemed to sink lower and lower.

Being stuck inside Jerusalem had made keeping my morning and afternoon appointments with God more difficult. Having people close by all the time made me long for the quiet of the fields around Anathoth and the peace of a solitary sunrise or sunset. The temple was the next best place to pray, but God's threat of destruction as repayment for the faithlessness practised within its walls[30] meant that I could not feel completely comfortable even there. Josiah had cleaned out all of the corruption he had found in God's house, but apparently his sons had brought idolatry back into the temple with a vengeance.

---

[30] Jeremiah 7:11-14; 26:6

During those winter months I found that I was not the only worshipper in the temple near sunrise. However, some of the people I met there surprised me a little. Several were men who showed little piety in their everyday life around the city, and I started to wonder what was going on. I watched them, hoping to see their true colours, and found that many of them seemed to show more interest in the sun than in the sanctuary. Then I suddenly remembered King Josiah sparking the destruction of the horses and chariots dedicated to the sun almost 25 years before, and wondered. Were men again coming to the temple of Yahweh to worship the sun?

For weeks I continued to watch them, which left me badly distracted from my own prayers; then one day I finally asked Azariah whether he knew anything about it. It was like speaking to my father all over again: the same answering without answering; the same justifying of the varied worship of others; the same lauding of tolerance and the need to seek a shared peace even amongst those who sought a different path from us. And sadly, his answers gave no consideration to Yahweh, the owner of the house, whose patience was being tried to breaking point by this spiritual adultery!

As I had feared, and indeed half-expected, we argued, and Azariah's anger matched my own, though it sprang from a different base. His was the anger of a custodian whose trustworthiness is questioned; the anger of a man who seeks peace at any cost, only to find that some consider the cost unacceptable.

He did not ask me to leave his house, but I left anyway. Some years previously, my younger cousin Hanamel had inherited a house in the city, and he and his wife welcomed me into it without question. Indeed, they carefully avoided discussing my reason for requesting their hospitality, since the High Priest could be a powerful enemy for a working priest like Hanamel – even if he was a close relative.

I continued to wonder about the future of Jeconiah's fledgling reign. His father and grandfather had each sat on the throne for years. Would he do the same, or would his reign be short, like that of his uncle Jehoahaz? And what of his mother – would she ever let him grow up and make his own decisions?

One day, I had enjoyed a time of evening prayer within the temple, and was still seeking answers to my questions about the future as I walked towards the gate. Suddenly, the gathering darkness seemed to lighten slightly, and immediately I knew what was happening. The presence of God was enveloping me, triggering the excitement and fear which his presence brings. Unaware of what I was doing, I fell to my knees on the paving just behind the gatehouse.

"As I live, declares the Lord,
though Coniah the son of Jehoiakim, king of Judah,
were the signet ring on my right hand,
yet I would tear you off and give you
into the hand of those who seek your life,
into the hand of those of whom you are afraid,
even into the hand of Nebuchadnezzar king of Babylon
and into the hand of the Chaldeans.
I will hurl you and the mother who bore you
into another country, where you were not born,
and there you shall die.
But to the land to which they will long to return,
there they shall not return."[31]

God's words were abrupt and the voice within me felt implacable, offering Jeconiah no hope. As God had promised Jehoahaz exile and an exile's death, so now he was promising Jeconiah the same fate. Yet in between, he

---

[31] Jeremiah 22:24-27

had allowed Jehoiakim to reign for 11 years – a reign filled with evil. I was reminded of the two object lessons that God had shown me through pottery: the first when a potter remade a pot that had been spoiled on the wheel before it was fired; the second highlighting the impossibility of fixing a fired pot once it has been shattered. Had Jehoahaz been more like a fired pot that had been broken? A man who was beyond fixing? Had Jehoiakim actually been more mouldable than his brother, a man with more potential? I felt that I had never seen any evidence of such potential – but I cannot see as God sees. And what about Jeconiah? The shortened form of his name was often used derisively by his detractors. Was that the reasoning behind God's use of it? As the overwhelming effects of God's voice slowly wore off, I was able to ask, "Is this man Coniah a despised, broken pot, a vessel no one cares for? Why are he and his children[32] hurled and cast into a land that they do not know?"[33]

God's answer was curt and did not completely answer my question:

"O land, land, land, hear the word of the Lord!
Thus says the Lord: 'Write this man down as childless,
a man who shall not succeed in his days,
for none of his offspring shall succeed
in sitting on the throne of David
and ruling again in Judah.' "[34]

---

[32] Jeconiah was only 18 years old at this time (see 2 Kings 24:8 and the note in Chapter 3 "Inside Jerusalem"), yet this passage in Jeremiah 22:28 refers to his children. Members of the royal family seem to have married at a very young age at this time. For example, King Jehoiakim was only 36 when he died, yet his son Jeconiah was already 18. It is possible that the reference to children is presuming that they would come, but it reads more as if they already existed.

[33] Jeremiah 22:28

[34] Jeremiah 22:29-30

So Jeconiah was to go into captivity and no son of his would reign on the throne of Judah. Once again, I jumped to conclusions and understood from God's words things that he had not said: that the kingdom of Judah would end with Jeconiah. Yet God had not said that, and it would not be long before my assumptions would be shown to be completely wrong.

Was God testing my understanding? I don't know for sure, but either way, his words finished abruptly and I found myself kneeling in the shadows of the gatekeepers' rooms as darkness continued to spread its veil over the city. A reverberating thud suddenly shook the earth from near Jeconiah's palace, reminding me that the Chaldeans were still outside the walls and their determination to overcome the city had not weakened.

What should I do with this message? Normally God told me what he wanted me to do, but this time he hadn't. Should I report God's words to the king? A few moments' thought removed my doubt: God's use of "you" when talking about Jeconiah meant that the words must be directed to him, so I must deliver them to him.

I climbed slowly to my feet and stretched, then went immediately to the gate of the palace, and approached one of the soldiers on guard, asking him to deliver a message from me to King Jeconiah. As we spoke, however, Ahikam, the son of Shaphan, also approached the gate and saw me.

"Jeremiah," he greeted me, "the Lord be with you."

"The Lord bless you," I answered absently, wondering if this was an opportunity to take advantage of Ahikam's newfound popularity with the king. But I didn't need to try.

"What are you doing here?" Ahikam asked me.

"God gave me a message for King Jeconiah," I replied. "I am trying to arrange a time to see him."

"Well, why don't you come in with me? I am about to go in to see the king to discuss our next steps in the defence of the city. Spring is beginning, the seasons are changing." He rubbed his hands together to warm them as he continued, "I can ask the king if he will give you an audience." We both knew that it was actually the queen mother's opinion that would decide the matter, but shared that knowledge with only a knowing glance and a slight smile. Diplomacy kept our lips sealed.

The guard let us pass and we climbed the steps into the palace. I had never been into the palace at night before and the corridors seemed dark and gloomy, despite the lamps that sat in niches along the walls. As Ahikam showed me into a waiting room near the throne room, he asked me, "The message for the king is not too bad, is it?" But before I could answer, the palace shook with a deep thud, closely followed by a spreading rumble as the sound of falling masonry came from somewhere above. Muffled shouts were followed by sudden screams, and Ahikam and I looked at each other uncertainly.

"That sounds serious," said Ahikam, worriedly, and left the room to investigate. I followed.

We were not the only ones responding to the alarming sounds. As we entered the corridor, we saw three guards hurrying out of the throne room. They turned away from us, ran towards a staircase and disappeared up it, taking two or three steps at a time. As we hurried towards the throne room, Jeconiah himself came out, looking afraid. By that time, the thunder of falling masonry from above had stopped, but the urgent shouting and periodic screams continued.

King Jeconiah saw Ahikam and immediately seemed to relax a little. Ahikam's presence had always had a calming effect when a situation was tense.

"Ah, Ahikam, you are here," said Jeconiah with relief. "What do you think the noise was?"

"I can't tell for sure, my lord," answered Ahikam, "but it sounded like a direct hit from a catapult somewhere on the roof. Probably some stonework has collapsed."

"Should we go up and look?" asked Jeconiah in agitation.

"No, I don't believe you should, my lord," advised Ahikam, coolly. "Others can assess the damage and you, as king, are best to stay away from the damaged areas. They may be dangerous, and we need to keep you safe!"

"Oh, I suppose so," conceded Jeconiah, pursing his lips in frustration. "But I would like to see up close what sort of damage these catapults can cause."

"Maybe you can look in the morning, my lord, after some stonemasons have looked at it and made sure it is safe."

King Jeconiah was just turning to re-enter the throne room when he saw me. "Jeremiah," he said in surprise, "what are you doing here?" Then, looking suddenly suspicious, he asked, "Is this damage your doing?"

"No, my lord, I wield no power like that," I replied. "I merely report the words of God. I am here because God has another message for you."

The king looked uncertain and glanced at Ahikam for guidance. Ahikam said nothing to sway his decision either way. He was probably wishing that he could have heard my answer to his question about the message I was to deliver.

By this time, the screaming had ceased, and only the occasional shout reminded us that the Chaldeans had been able to deliver death and destruction even within the king's palace.

For a few moments of indecision, Jeconiah looked from Ahikam to me and back again. Then he replied, "Very well, come in and we will hear what you have to say. Ahikam will be able to give us his advice, too."

The king turned and entered the throne room through the door used by his subjects, a fact which highlighted how disturbed he had been by the direct hit from the Chaldean catapult and its immediate aftermath. It was unheard of for the king to enter or leave his throne room through the same door as his subjects! Nehushta would not be pleased with him.

Ahikam followed the king, and I followed Ahikam. As I entered the room, one of the guards who had gone up to investigate the incident on the roof slipped into the throne room behind me.

He stood silently, waiting to be questioned, but was obviously full of news. Nehushta was standing on the dais near her chair, waiting for the king to take his seat. As King Jeconiah sat down on his throne, he saw the guard and prompted him, "What happened?"

"A direct hit from a very large rock, sir," said the guard excitedly. "It hit the parapet around the roof and broke it down – there's rubble everywhere. Some of the scattered stones from the parapet fell down the stairway that leads into the palace and two men on the floor below were badly injured. The rock that broke through the parapet then hit the small building on the roof, the one next to the altar that your father built. The wall collapsed and the roof of the building fell in on the four men who were inside. Two of them were killed outright by the rock and the wall together, while the other two were badly injured by a heavy beam which fell on them. The beam landed right on top of them both and one of them had his head…"

He was obviously going to give more gory details, but Nehushta interrupted. "Enough! We don't need to hear any more. Has the damage made any parts of the palace unsafe?"

"I'm sorry, ma'am, but we don't know yet. A stonemason has been sent for, but until he comes, we really don't know. But the two men who were hit by the beam, they are very…"

"That will do," said Nehushta, holding up an imperious hand, her tone brooking no opposition.

The guard subsided and returned to his position beside the door, looking a little disappointed. Nehushta sat down regally upon her chair and waited for her son to speak.

"Now, Jeremiah, tell us your message," said King Jeconiah, and his mother looked around with a start. She had obviously not noticed my entrance in front of the eager guard. Jeconiah glanced across at her, looking rather pleased with himself for having slipped me into the room without his mother noticing.

"What is he doing here?" asked Nehushta.

"He has a message from Yahweh for us," replied Jeconiah. "I thought we should hear it."

"Very well, Coniah," she replied dubiously, "if that is what you want."

I approached the dais at the front of the room. King Jeconiah looked more at home on the throne than he had when I had first met him. But though two months had given him more confidence, the commanding presence on the dais was still his mother. She was dressed in long flowing robes, richly embroidered with purple and blue and also with threads of pure gold. Above the hem of her skirt, the sun, moon and stars formed a wide background on which gods and goddesses cavorted in their imagined triumphs. Her striking red hair was elaborately arranged; combs and jewelled pins shaped it into a tower that looked very imposing. However, her physical beauty was more than outweighed by the scowl that had settled on her face when she recognised me. Would she have allowed me to enter if Jeconiah had asked her opinion?

Ignoring her glowering face, I addressed myself to her son – after all, he was meant to be the king!

"O king," I began, "Yahweh our God has given me a message that you need to hear." Then I carefully repeated the words of God to them. How they burned within me – each letter flaming brightly on the wall of my mind, particularly as I spoke the words:

"I will hurl you and the mother who bore you
into another country, where you were not born,
and there you shall die."

I was looking at King Jeconiah as I spoke, because the words were addressed to him, but Nehushta interrupted angrily: "These are not the words of a god. These are your words. The words of a traitor!"

"My lady, these are indeed the words of Yahweh, the God of Israel, and he continues…" I repeated the curse God had laid on Jeconiah, that none of his children would succeed in sitting on the throne of David. Thankfully, Nehushta did not interrupt again.

After I finished, there was silence for a while. Would they take this message seriously? If they did, what would they do about it? Jeconiah was stroking his thin beard again and seemed to be wondering what to do next. He looked at his mother for guidance, but she only kept scowling at me. Then he looked helplessly at Ahikam, who, after a few moments, rescued him.

"My lord," said Ahikam confidently, "Jeremiah's words should be considered carefully. Yahweh anointed your father, King David, as king to replace Saul, the son of Kish. He promised that David would always have a son to sit on his throne if his sons obeyed his commands. Many generations have passed. Some kings have strayed from David's ways, but God has always been faithful and forgiving. God is warning you, as he has warned kings throughout our history, that you must not ignore him completely."

"So how much attention should we pay to Jeremiah's words?" asked Jeconiah.

"How important is your life and your dynasty, my lord?" countered Ahikam.

"But the words of Yahweh directly condemn me and my children to exile and death. Why do you imply that there is a choice to be made?"

I had been wondering that myself! Where was Ahikam leading the king?

"Our God is a forgiving God. Repentance will always touch his heart."

Ahikam was advising the king to repent, and Jeconiah was listening to his advice. Even Nehushta had a look of doubt on her face. I was breathless with excitement as I listened to the discussion, which continued as if I were not there.

Ahikam led the conversation carefully. A wise man, he always acknowledged Jeconiah first, as king, while tailoring his arguments to convince Nehushta.

After some time, Jeconiah seemed to notice me again and said, "Jeremiah, we will consider your words, and consult with Ahikam regarding what we should do. In the meantime, you may go."

I left the room, led by the guard Nehushta had silenced, and we walked down the corridor to the front of the palace.

"I wonder how those poor fellows are," the guard mused as we walked. "That was a mighty heavy beam… and right on their heads, too. I don't think they will be recovering in a hurry."

"I don't think they will be the last victims of this siege," I said, and walked down the steps out of the palace.

CR

I spoke to Ahikam the next day to see what had emerged from his discussions with King Jeconiah and Nehushta. His son Gedaliah was with him as we talked, and seeing the two of them together reminded me of Shaphan and Ahikam when I was first speaking God's words in Jerusalem. They had made a very capable father and son pairing: the father powerful and influential, and the son walking steadily in his father's footsteps. In those days, I had never met either of them, although my father had known them both well. To me, they were part of the group of "six mysterious men"[35] who had come several times to listen to my words, but left soon afterwards without talking to me. Once we had finally begun to talk and I had got to know them somewhat, I had learned to respect their serious, enquiring minds and brilliant ability to assess the state of the kingdom and give good advice. Gedaliah was the next generation, about 30 years old in the time of Jeconiah and showing signs of being another from the same mould. He deferred to his father, as you might expect, and seemed eager to learn at any opportunity.

The family was known for its careful blending of an inclination towards Yahweh with a pragmatism that had helped Shaphan to begin a brilliant career even before Josiah became king. Ahikam had been denied some of that success due to his prominent involvement during the reign of Josiah: King Jehoiakim had always viewed with displeasure any of the men who had been popular with his father.

---

[35] See Volume 1 – Early Days, Chapters 4 and 9.

Gedaliah was benefitting from the family's prominence in the kingdom, and showed great promise in civic leadership.

He contributed to our discussion about how Jeconiah should respond to God's curse, agreeing with his father that repentance was necessary. Naturally I agreed, but we differed as to the shape and scope of that repentance. Once again, pragmatism was in conflict with idealism. My expressed wish that both the king and the queen mother should abandon their worship of other gods and serve Yahweh alone was thought by both to be an unreasonable, impractical demand.

Should I have been pleased that they wanted some repentance or furious that the repentance they advocated was too little, too late?

Ahikam said that both Jeconiah and Nehushta had received advice from others that they should surrender to Nebuchadnezzar if they could obtain any guarantee of gentle treatment. This sounded to me like a reasonable option, so I was surprised when Ahikam added that he had advised them not even to consider such an option.

"Why?" I asked, blankly.

"Babylon is a cruel nation," said Ahikam. "You told us so just before they attacked Jerusalem the first time,[36] and they proved you right. Would you really believe any guarantee they offered?"

"I would believe God's guarantee that King Jeconiah will be given into their hands, so fighting them isn't going to change the result. Surely the only thing that might change it is genuine, determined repentance, isn't it?"

"But we can't just give up so easily," argued Ahikam. "Surely we could try some negotiation, some targeted resistance, couldn't we?"

---

[36] Jeremiah 6:23

"Be careful who you oppose, my friend," I responded. "If you're not careful, you will find yourself opposing Yahweh."

"Oh, no, I wouldn't do anything like that. You know how important our God is to me."

He was right, I did. But I also knew how important admiration was to him, and how irresistible he found the challenge of giving compelling advice that people would admire.

℞

Nebuchadnezzar had spent some time dealing with Egypt. Ahikam and I discussed what Nebuchadnezzar's plans might be and it was fascinating to listen to his incisive assessment of what we could expect. In his opinion, Nebuchadnezzar had decided not to attack in sufficient force to defeat this long-time superpower, declining though it was, because he could not afford the drain on his resources that subjugating Egypt would demand. Rather, his aim would probably be to build a frontier, a barrier to keep Pharaoh inside his own land and under control. Ahikam believed Nebuchadnezzar wanted Judah as the boundary of his empire – for the time being at least – and would do his best to teach Egypt to keep out. Two months had been spent in this endeavour, and, based on the latest information from Jeconiah's scouts, Nebuchadnezzar had left some troops to guard the border, and was now working his way north, attacking and destroying many of the southern cities of Judah. Within weeks, Ahikam said, we could expect Nebuchadnezzar to reach Jerusalem with reinforcements to help his besieging army conquer the city.

Throughout the twelfth month,[37] as winter gradually came to an end but the rains continued to fall, King Jeconiah continued to withstand the army of Nebuchadnezzar that was outside the walls.

Within Jerusalem, water supplies were holding up – well, of course they were, it was still the wet season! Food reserves were not yet becoming critical, but there were deepening shortages. Far less food was available within the city than would have been the case if the siege had been expected. Even Jeconiah and his mother were suffering a little under the shortages brought about by the siege – only half of the palace lights were being lit each night, due to the limited supplies of olive oil available within the walls.

Yet Jeconiah showed no visible signs of repentance and it seemed that Ahikam had scuttled the idea of surrender.

My prayers had been so mixed up over the years: begging forgiveness and demanding punishment; seeking God's patience and asking for urgent action. But surely this siege must be the time of the end? God's prophecies must be culminating in a climactic and terrible end. Weeks, or possibly only days, were all the time that remained for the temple courts in which I often prayed. The dreadful conclusion promised for Jerusalem and God's own house filled me with terror.

But my family: what of them? What would happen to my mother? My brothers and their families? Zaccai and Abigail; Ahikam and his family; Meshullam; Ezekiel; relatives, friends and acquaintances; potters, blacksmiths and metalworkers; even my enemies? I knew that we and our fathers had sinned, but I could not abandon them all to utter destruction. Nevertheless, God had forbidden me

---

[37] Late February and early March.

to pray for my people,[38] so all I could do was urge repentance. God would be more likely to listen to a real, active repentance. My prayers must be limited to prayers for courage, wisdom and the right choice of words. Would God spare them? Would he spare me?

Then suddenly everything changed.

March, 597 BC – the 3rd month of King Jeconiah

Nebuchadnezzar arrived from the south in great splendour, with an army even greater than the one already camped outside our walls. A flurry of diplomacy followed: offers, demands and concessions; and then abruptly King Jeconiah and his mother surrendered, and Nebuchadnezzar, the king of Babylon, was king of Jerusalem too.

---

[38] Jeremiah 7:16; 11:14; 14:11

Chapter 7

Nebuchadnezzar decides

Ahikam stood firm to the end against the idea of surrendering. His oft-stated reason was that the Chaldeans could not be trusted, but an unguarded comment the night before the king surrendered showed that this was not his only reason.

"I don't like the idea of surrendering, Jeremiah," he said. "It may seem like a good idea to you, but for the first time in several years, I am back in a position to advise the king and try to help the kingdom return more to how it was under Josiah. If we surrender, all of that will be placed in jeopardy. I have had such a short time to try!"

However, his advice to King Jeconiah was ignored. Strangely enough, I think it was God's warning that he would give Jeconiah into the hand of Nebuchadnezzar and send him into exile that won the day. Despite Jeconiah's evil and idolatrous attitude, he still had a sneaking feeling that God's prophecies would come true. It was probably the first time in his life that he made an important decision himself rather than following his mother's lead. Nehushta was not utterly opposed to the surrender, but she was certainly concerned, and would have continued to resist just to avoid the immediate risk.

In looking back over the years, I wonder if it was Jeconiah's willingness to make that decision and surrender – to stop fighting against what God had said – that caused him to be treated so gently by King Nebuchadnezzar. Yes, he was taken away to Babylon, and still lives in exile, but he went with his wives and his children and has been treated quite kindly.

ↂ

On the day that Nebuchadnezzar arrived with his army, riding in a splendid chariot and surrounded by a retinue of splendidly-dressed nobles, Jeconiah was immediately advised of the new development.

That evening, Ahikam told me that Jeconiah had remembered my words, with their warning that he would be handed over to Nebuchadnezzar who sought his life. His life hung in doubt before him and he saw only one possible way out – surrender.

Ahikam told me that he had tried to convince the king that nothing had really changed, and that King Nebuchadnezzar's appearance made no difference. They had been enduring a siege yesterday and they would continue to endure it today, and tomorrow as well.

Nehushta seemed almost convinced by Ahikam's arguments, but Jeconiah was not. Instead, he wanted advice about how he could send a message to Nebuchadnezzar to sound him out about possible options for ending the siege. Ahikam seemed rather disappointed as he told me that he had continued trying to convince the king, but that King Jeconiah had soon called other councillors and dispatched them to seek a parley with

King Nebuchadnezzar, while Ahikam himself had been dismissed.

Nebuchadnezzar had been very willing to parley, although he had given little away. The siege had already cost many Chaldean lives and more than three months of wages and other expenses. Rebel states must not be allowed to offer such extended resistance without punishment. However, if he offered the defenders nothing, the siege might continue for months or years.

Both parties negotiated cannily and each got some of what they wanted. Agreement was close by sunset, and finally, late in the evening, a messenger from King Jeconiah took Nebuchadnezzar the news that the king would surrender in the morning with his family, his advisors, his nobles and his officers.

As we sat and talked far into the evening, Ahikam explained what Jeconiah was attempting. A series of messages came from the palace making the direction of the negotiations clear, and Ahikam looked a little more resigned as each messenger arrived.

At last, just as I was leaving Ahikam's grand home that night, a messenger came to report the final agreement, and Ahikam knew that he had lost. In just a few hours, the city would be in Chaldean hands. His short-lived recall as a royal advisor had come to an end.

Later that night, as a sign of good faith, Nebuchadnezzar's catapults ceased delivering their metered doses of death. Yet such was the fear that they had already generated that they still haunted the dreams of many.

Few of those who were to leave the comparative safety of the city walls the next morning slept much that night. Those who surrender risk much, and many of those who were to join the capitulating group in the morning had little confidence in King Nebuchadnezzar's word. As for

Chaldean mercy – why, everyone had heard stories of their brutality, a brutality which had outshone even the cruelty of the vicious Assyrians in its heartlessness.

But what choice was there? A protracted siege, however long it might last, would still have to end sometime, and by then the king would have no bargaining chips left to offer the vengeful attackers.

The shortage of lamp oil meant that many in Jerusalem were already asleep as the finishing touches were put on the plan that would surrender them all to the dubious kindness of the Chaldeans. For them, the morning would be soon enough to hear the frightening news.

However, among those who were wakeful in the night hours – the sick or injured and those who tended them; those giving birth to the next generation; those who must keep watch over the city for one more night; and those who were drowning their worries with wine – the news spread quickly. The terror that had so long crouched, waiting, outside the walls, was to be unleashed among them in just a few hours.

I spent most of the night in prayer, with only tiny snatches of sleep. I was not allowed to pray for my nation, but surely prayer for my family and friends would be acceptable to God? Finally, well before dawn, I made my way to the temple, longing for one last look at its beauty before this house of God was reduced to rubble, like the ruin that had been Shiloh.

Morning came with a dull grey light that reflected the mood in the city. Those who had not already heard the news heard it then as it spread from mouth to mouth. Many were woken by a neighbour's urgent knock on the door, and stumbled from their beds only to hear the unwelcome news.

Before the dullness of dawn had lightened many shades, the news was all over the city, and everyone had to decide what to do with the time that remained.

Those with valuables still left to hide, hid them. Some cleaned their houses, just for something to do. Many began to prepare special feasts, eager to use the best of their carefully preserved stores before they became spoil for the Chaldeans.

Those who had nothing to do spent the time in fear.

Children born during the night, whose lives could well be snuffed out before they had ever really begun, were fed by new mothers who gloried in their new babies' perfect features and tiny hands, yet dreaded what the day would bring to those defenceless treasures.

Numbly, the people made their preparations. But what can one do to prepare for a future that is so uncertain?

The king and his mother had worked throughout the night with their advisors and scribes, making lists. By morning, the list of people who would walk through the gate with them to meet the waiting representatives of their conqueror was complete. Nobles and important officials, favoured servants and guards were listed one by one. Ahikam was on the list. Surprisingly, Azariah, my brother, was not.

Nebuchadnezzar had promised that none of these people would be immediately injured or killed – unless they caused particular trouble.

Azariah was on the second list, the list of those who would meet King Nebuchadnezzar when he entered the city. Gedaliah was on this list too, along with various others who were thought to be important enough – and who were gifted with silver tongues. The royal wives and children would also greet the conqueror in humble acknowledgement of his sovereignty over them.

Other lists included the names of rich men and leaders, soldiers, archers, watchmen and gatekeepers, artisans and metalworkers. Nebuchadnezzar had demanded these lists and had indicated that the men included would not be killed, but would probably be taken away into captivity.

I was not on any list.

Throughout the city, preparations for the surrender continued. Dress and personal presentation demanded particular attention. Many men dressed in their best finery, while others chose to dress in worn clothes, cultivating an appearance well below their station in life: guessing and second-guessing what appearance would give the best hope of survival.

Women likewise prepared for the day with great care. Some dressed splendidly, hoping that beauty or elegance would win them notice and protection, while others did their best to hide any physical beauty that God had given them, seeking to make themselves appear plain and unattractive in the hope that they would remain unnoticed, should the violence and lust of a victorious army be let loose on the vanquished.

Within the temple, all was frantic activity. On his first "visit", Nebuchadnezzar had taken away many of the special utensils, implements and other valuables from the temple. Plenty of gold and silver cups and other vessels had gone with him to Babylon, and the priests did not want that to happen again. Some of the treasures had been replaced over the intervening years, as worshippers gave gifts, but most of these were not as grand as the items that had been taken last time. Thus, the High Priest was determined that as much of the treasure as possible should be hidden. The work of concealment had begun shortly after the Chaldean army had first arrived, but many of the objects that had been in daily use would now be hidden as well. Of course, it was a fine line to walk;

the temple must still look like a fully-functioning place of worship, with no hint that items had been removed and secreted. Many vessels must be left in place, even some of the most valuable, but the very best must be hidden in places where they would never be found.

Underneath the temple pavements were tunnels and channels for both drainage and water storage. Within this network of dark places, carefully wrapped objects were concealed: not too many in one place together, lest a chance discovery reveal too much, yet not in too many places either, lest one be found by accident and trigger a more thorough search. Guess and second-guess, conceal and reveal. Clumsy hiding places were chosen too, to give the impression of last-minute, hurried, amateurish, concealment; the hint that a cursory search would be enough to find all of the treasures available.

In the palace, and in fact, all over the city, people were playing the same high-risk game, while outside the city, the soldiers were dreaming of the valuables that the day would put into their hands.

Through all of these preparations flowed undercurrents of terror, surfacing from time to time in public anger and violence, but mostly cloaked in a quiet resignation. No-one knew what the day would bring, and the situation was beyond their control.

It was mid-morning before the preparations were complete and the royal party was assembled at the Benjamin Gate, ready for their appointment with uncertainty. King Jeconiah was to lead the way, with his personal servants, and his mother would follow, leading the nobles and senior officials.

I watched as the group assembled, and then climbed to the top of the wall. A prophet is sometimes allowed to do things that ordinary citizens would not get away with, and I was allowed to stand among the men of war and watch the developments outside the gate. As I stood next to an archer, he filled me in on the events that I had missed.

During the morning, the Chaldeans had set up a large, brightly decorated tent outside the gate, beyond the tattered remnants of faded cloth that covered the remains of what had once been King Jehoiakim. A constant stream of workers had set up its posts and coverings, then brought provisions for what seemed likely to be a sumptuous feast. Flags fluttered from its corners and many guards surrounded it. The work of preparation seemed to have come to an end. All was ready. One of the guards carried a trumpet and, at a signal from his commander, he put the instrument to his lips and blew a signal of truce. This was the signal King Jeconiah had been waiting for. Hostilities would formally pause if the defenders acknowledged the signal, and the king motioned to his trumpeter, who blew a confirming blast on his shofar.

A group of men of military appearance, but apparently unarmed and with only a few guards, walked past the tent and moved along the road towards the gate.

At the same time, the gates of Jerusalem were slowly opened and a young man walked nervously out from under the archway. He wore a king's crown and was closely followed by attendants, as befitted his station in life. A few paces behind him, a woman walked with stately tread, her auburn tresses piled up on her head in a beehive shape, held by a multitude of jewelled pins and decorated combs. A golden tiara encircled her head and her clothing was elegant, but restrained. A step behind her walked Ahikam and the rest of king Jeconiah's advisors, as well as the city administrators and other officials from the palace.

Archers and slingers watched from the wall, bows carefully slung across their shoulders and slings out of sight.   No accidental shooting of an arrow or other threatening action could be allowed to endanger this ceasefire.

The company walked from the gate towards the welcoming party of Chaldeans. No smiles lit up the faces of either party as they would have for a meeting of friends. Instead, they appeared to be schooled to carefully avoid any expression at all.

After what seemed like a very long, slow walk, the two groups met. From the wall, we could hear the occasional murmur of voices, but nothing more. Everyone waited anxiously to see if events would go smoothly, and for a time all appeared to be going well.

The two parties walked together towards the large tent where a man stood waiting, backed by a large crowd of attendants and people who looked as if they must be advisors. Their dress suggested great importance. On either side of the man stood two enormous warriors in full armour with drawn swords – obviously bodyguards, ready for any treachery that might arise.

"King Nebuchadnezzar, I think," said the archer next to me, pointing to the man who stood waiting. Thus it was that I had my first glimpse of the man whose glorious empire would soon overrun all of the nations around about.

The tent had been set up beyond the range of any archer or slinger who might seek glory for himself by killing the king of Babylon, so those of us who watched from the wall had only a distant view of the events that followed as King Jeconiah greeted Nebuchadnezzar. We saw our king bowing down with his face to the ground before Nebuchadnezzar, and the latter taking him by the hand and lifting him up. Next, the queen mother and then Ahikam and the other nobles and officials approached Nebuchadnezzar one by one and bowed down before him in the same way, though Jeconiah was the only one he extended his hand to.

Once the initial greetings were over, Nebuchadnezzar appeared to be interrogating Jeconiah, and he seemed angry at times. Ahikam seemed to be drawn into the conversation briefly, and then suddenly Nebuchadnezzar stepped back and signalled furiously to two bodyguards. Jeconiah jumped back hurriedly as the guards moved forward, and only Ahikam remained standing where he was. The guard on Nebuchadnezzar's right took the lead, lifting his sword as he walked toward Ahikam. The curved sword rose briefly in the air before slashing downwards with frightening speed. Ahikam stood unmoving until the blade caught him and cut him down. Then both guards stood over him and their swords ran red with blood.

There was no more violence during that interview with King Nebuchadnezzar, and later inquiries showed that it had resulted from Ahikam's repeated attempts to convince King Jeconiah not to surrender. Nebuchadnezzar had asked Jeconiah to explain why he had continued to resist, and why he and all of his household should not be killed. Jeconiah, terrified, had begun to claim that he had wanted to surrender all along but that his advisors had told him not to. He was quick to state that Ahikam, who was standing right behind him, was the strongest advocate against surrendering. Nebuchadnezzar was furious, and waited only to confirm with Ahikam that this was true before ordering his execution. Ahikam may have had a strong yearning for power, but he had always told the truth.

So it was that Ahikam was the first casualty of the peace, but he was by no means the last. I still miss his incisive comments and his loyal friendship. A desire for power will often betray us.

Jeconiah and his party were invited to enter the splendid tent soon after Ahikam had been hacked to death. As they disappeared into the tent, we watchers on the wall wondered if we would ever see them alive again. At first, many stayed to watch, but as time passed, most lost patience and left, until only the soldiers remained, still feeling that it was their duty to do so.

For myself, after waiting and watching for quite a long time, I descended the steps from the wall and returned to the temple. I still expected Nebuchadnezzar to enter the city shortly and begin the utter destruction God had promised – and I had no idea what would happen to me. God had promised to care for me during my prophesying, but maybe the end of my prophesying had come. After all, if Judah was to be destroyed, what need would there be for prophets?

I went to my favourite place in the temple, a quiet area where there were no grand surroundings and no priests carefully attending me – and no hidden idols either. On normal days, it was a place where I could spend time with God and think back over my work, while wondering about the future; a place of calm.

But this was no ordinary day, and there didn't seem to be any place in the temple that was calm! Priests and Levites were standing in groups, talking worriedly, while worshippers wailed and called on their gods – and most of them were not calling on Yahweh. The names of Baal, Asherah, Molech, Milcom, Tammuz and even the sun, moon and many of the stars of the heavens were echoing through the courts of the temple, the very temple which Solomon had built to the glory of Yahweh, the God of Israel, the God who is one God, the only God.

If God's temple was like this, what were the other parts of the city like? Other parts of the city were even more prone to the worship of foolish idols, so what would I find there?

Leaving the temple, I went to the Potsherd Gate, where the broken and spoiled pottery was piling up against the wall. Nebuchadnezzar's army had cut off access to the valley outside, and emptying large piles of shards right outside the wall would just have made it easier for the Chaldeans to build siege ramps against the wall, so a jumbled mound of broken pieces had grown up inside the wall in the area around the gate. Until the previous day, potters had still been working, although no new supplies of clay had been brought into the city for more than three months. But today was different: no-one was working. The potter whose working and re-working of a pot God had instructed me to watch so long ago – could it really be eleven years ago? – sat at his booth and talked to his neighbours. Concentrating on any work was beyond everyone, but how do you prepare for an army to overrun your city? During the siege, most people had hidden everything that was particularly valuable to them, so on this morning when the siege was ending, they were left with nothing to do but wait and worry – and call upon whatever gods they worshipped. Fear intruded on every conversation and no-one knew quite what to do.

But no-one was lining up to offer last-ditch repentance to God. Jerusalem was not a pot that could be reshaped. Instead, it was a hardened, fired pot, fixed in its twisted and corrupt appearance before God: impossible to reshape, impossible to soften. The hard hearts of young and old, rich and poor, men and women alike were all rigid in their rejection of God's demands.

I returned to the Benjamin Gate, and Nebuchadnezzar rode into the city soon after, at the head of a massive column of soldiers. Jeconiah was not with him. He was to stay in the custody of the Chaldean army until King Nebuchadnezzar decided what to do with him.

Nebuchadnezzar's attendants had with them Jeconiah's lists of the people of importance in the city. These lists had taken a large group of scribes all of the previous night to complete, and they included the names of all of the city officials, the nobles and rich men, the soldiers in the city, and all the craftsmen and metal workers.

Gradually it became clear that all of the men on the lists were being systematically rounded up and collected in the open squares of the city and in the temple courts. They came with their wives and their children, clutching a pitifully few belongings. I watched from the gates of the temple and saw many men whom I knew as they walked uncertainly to join the others already assembling in the open areas in front of the temple, and in the temple courts themselves. The potter whom I had seen just a short while before was leading a young boy by one hand while a woman followed clutching a small baby to her breast. Two young girls walked with them. Fear was in all their faces, although the potter tried bravely to hide it.

I felt completely left out. Nobody was interested in me. I had no position that made me important, no money or desirable trade that would indicate ability. I was one of the poor, the ordinary. I was not even dangerous enough to be worth gathering among the worthwhile citizens of Jerusalem, those who might pose a threat to Nebuchadnezzar's control in the city.

All these would be taken to Babylon as captives.

I would be left behind.

But the option to stay or go tells only a part of the story of what unfolded that day in Jerusalem. Thousands of Chaldean soldiers moved through the city with swords unsheathed and spears at the ready. Before long, the sword and spears had been bathed in blood and thousands of the men and women of Judah had been slaughtered. I lost several friends in the bloodbath. Worst of all, Zaccai and Abigail would never again give me news of Daniel and his friends: they died violently at the hands of soldiers eager for loot.

But some considered that the ones who had died were the lucky ones: others stayed alive through the abuse of a flood of soldiers freed from restraint.

So much destruction; yet the utter desolation that I had expected did not occur. Jerusalem was spared. The temple was looted, but not destroyed. The ten thousand men appointed for deportation were marched out of the city along with their women and children to spend the night amongst the tents of the Chaldean army. Then, once the temple courts had been cleared, all of the golden artefacts and items of silver were brought triumphantly out of their storerooms and hiding places and piled up on the pavement. Intricately decorated golden cups and tongs, snuffers and many other items were thrown roughly in heaps while Chaldean labourers used hammers and mallets to crush them into more regularly shaped bricks of gold that would be easier to transport to Babylon. Gold was taken as gold, and silver as silver. The beauty and artistry in their fine designs disappeared beneath the crushing blows, and objects preserved for centuries disappeared into sacks ready for transportation to Nebuchadnezzar's treasury.

Some others who had not appeared on any of the lists were taken too. I saw Ezekiel and his wife among the throng in the temple courts, standing patiently, waiting for the word of command that would begin their long journey to Babylon.

I remember that day as clearly as if it had been yesterday. I have tried to retell its events briefly and simply, but it was a day of terror and horror. Tears stained many faces amongst the captives, and flowed freely among those who would be left, falling unnoticed on pavements and chairs, or onto floors stained with blood. They mourned the friends and family who would never return, and they mourned the dead whose fears for that day had come true.

Yet this day was as nothing compared to the day that would come in just eleven more years. On that day, all my fears of desolation were not only fulfilled, but exceeded – beyond my worst imaginings.

Already, sin and faithlessness were earning their reward, but worse was yet to come.

Chapter 8

What is left?

Thousands of Chaldean soldiers stayed in the city that night. They filled up some of the empty houses, but many also roamed around looking for trouble, and by the end of the night, even more houses had no living inhabitants.

Those doomed to exile slept, if they slept at all, without any protection from the cold of the night, herded into walled compounds that had been built by the Chaldean army to protect their soldiers from wild animals and the threat of attacks from within the city. Fires burned brightly all night, and soldiers kept a close watch on the captives in the compounds. I slept very little myself that night, held within Hanamel's house by a night-time curfew imposed by the Chaldean soldiers, but kept awake by the question: what would happen next? When would God's promised destruction come on Jerusalem?

Nebuchadnezzar was apparently in a hurry to depart: he left with his entourage the very next day, accompanied by a large force of mounted soldiers, travelling north. His decision about Jeconiah's future was not yet known.

Possibly he wished to consult with his army commanders in the north before making a final decision. Or maybe he was just playing games, preferring to keep people in anxious uncertainty.

Whatever the reason, in the meantime, Jeconiah would stay in custody outside the city.

The next day was a perfect early spring day. The sun shone warmly from a clear sky, and birds flitted over a city which was still largely in shock. Yet much of the action that day was not inside the city, but outside, where the Jewish prisoners were gradually coming to terms with their new status – slaves beneath the lowest of the Chaldeans' existing slaves.

Nebuchadnezzar's plan was to take the prisoners to Babylon and distribute them to areas where they would be useful to the empire. But before their long journey could begin, each person must be shackled, to ensure that there would be no escapes along the way. This process would take several weeks, and during that time, the Chaldeans would also begin to provide tents for the multitude of captives.

Sadly, shackling the prisoners seemed to be a higher priority for the Chaldean commanders than the provision of tents, and it took the best part of a week before any tents at all began to appear in the prisoners' compounds. During that week, the rain fell liberally on two days and the captives could only endure the discomfort. At other times, sunshine was plentiful, so the wet clothing usually dried quickly. But when the rain fell in the cold darkness of night, there was little to relieve the suffering of the men, women and children who huddled together trying to keep warm.

I couldn't help remembering the words of God in the Book of the Law, where God had promised us suffering if we did not obey his commands:

> "Because you did not serve the Lord your God
> with joyfulness and gladness of heart,
> because of the abundance of all things,
> therefore you shall serve your enemies
> whom the Lord will send against you,
> in hunger and thirst, in nakedness,
> and lacking everything.
> And he will put a yoke of iron on your neck
> until he has destroyed you.
> The Lord will bring a nation against you
> from far away, from the end of the earth,
> swooping down like the eagle,
> a nation whose language you do not understand,
> a hard-faced nation who shall not respect the old
> or show mercy to the young."[39]

Some years earlier, God had made me wear a yoke of wood as his prophet,[40] but a yoke of iron was what he had promised to our nation if we would not serve him and rejoice in all the blessings he gave. So now, metal bands were being forged around the necks and ankles of God's people because we had reserved our joy and gladness for the self-indulgent and depraved worship of idols.

No doubt the exiles would quickly learn Aramaic, urged on by the cruel commands of a hard-faced nation – just as God had warned so long ago. Would the captives learn that it was better to serve God in joy and happiness than to serve men in suffering? Or would they just blame God for all of their distress?

Inside the city, most of the people who remained were poor and unskilled. A few rich people had been left, along with some who would become leaders. It was hard to understand the reasoning behind why some were taken and others left.

---

[39] Deuteronomy 28:47-50

[40] Jeremiah 27 (see also Volume 3 – Darkness Falling, Chapter 11)

I was very pleased that my mother had been left in peace and still remained in the city. My prayers had been very urgent, and God had answered them. God had forbidden me from praying for the nation, and I had obeyed him in that, but I had prayed fervently for some individuals during that long night before Jeconiah surrendered. I hoped – and genuinely believed – that God's ban referred to the sorts of prayer for intercession which Moses had prayed for the entire nation.

Azariah, my brother, was the most powerful leader in what should have been our national religion, yet he remained. I could only assume that the Chaldeans believed that he would give them better cooperation than any replacement they could find.

My brother Gemariah remained likewise, and Ahikam's son Gedaliah too. Even Ahikam's brother, Elasah, was left. Once again, they may have been seen as people who could lead the nation in cooperation with their new masters.

My cousin Hanamel and his wife and children remained also.

Unoccupied houses were everywhere, their owners having been taken away or killed, but no-one was allowed to move into them at first. Instead, the Chaldean commanders spread their men through many of the empty houses, and the night-time curfew continued.

Theoretically, we were allowed to move about the city during the day, but there were checkpoints everywhere, manned by belligerent soldiers who were looking for trouble. It was safer to stay indoors, but even then, you might be found by groups of soldiers who were always searching for men to press into service carrying the booty they had gathered to places outside the city, where it was all packed into carts ready to be carried back to Babylon.

The violence meted out by the Chaldean soldiers was decreasing, but if a soldier gave you an instruction, you were wise to obey quickly, as it made no difference to him whether you lived or died. Others would learn to be quicker to obey if grudging obedience earned a sudden death.

But the widespread violence and destruction which I had expected did not come to the city. Any houses that burned down seemed to have been set alight by mistake, and no wanton destruction followed.

I waited and watched in expectation, but slowly began to understand that my expectations were not to be fulfilled. Of course, it could all change very quickly with a simple order from King Nebuchadnezzar, but it seemed that the soldiers were not expecting to destroy the temple or Jerusalem itself.

In the end, the only important order that arrived from Nebuchadnezzar was that Jeconiah was to be sent to Babylon, with his mother and his family. Nebuchadnezzar would be going to Babylon immediately, and he wanted Jeconiah and the other captives to meet him there as soon as possible.

The real surprise was that the same order appointed a new king. Mattaniah was a prince who had been left behind by history, or so it had seemed. A younger son of Josiah, he had been only ten years old when his father had died at the hand of Pharaoh Neco. His mother was Hamutal, the daughter of Jeremiah of Libnah,[41] whose oldest son, Jehoahaz, had been taken away to Egypt by Pharaoh Neco when he had returned from his battles in the north.

Mattaniah was now plucked from obscurity and appointed king. In fact, he had to be fetched from one of

---

[41] 2 Kings 24:18

the compounds outside the city where he had been waiting for a metal collar of his own along with the other captives.

But it wasn't quite as straightforward as it sounds. Apparently 21-year-old Mattaniah was first taken to Nebuchadnezzar's supreme commander and given a stern talking to. He was told that Nebuchadnezzar's original intention had been to put an end to the kingdom of Judah, instead appointing a governor who would be closely supervised by Chaldean officers. However, he had decided to show mercy and allow the nation to retain a king – Mattaniah himself – as long as he would agree to certain conditions. Nebuchadnezzar believed that an Israelite who took an oath in the name of Yahweh could be trusted to keep a covenant. Maybe he was swayed in that by the behaviour he had seen amongst the captives already in Babylon, men like Daniel and his friends. Of course, he should have been right.

Mattaniah would need to agree to steer the kingdom along humble lines; not rebelling against Nebuchadnezzar himself, nor seeking to build a coalition of nations to resist Babylon.

The commander emphasised to Mattaniah that Nebuchadnezzar had specified these conditions personally, and had also given a promise on oath that if Mattaniah would agree to the conditions, the kingdom of Judah would continue to have a king. This was the covenant Nebuchadnezzar offered to Mattaniah – as well as requirements for the payment of tribute money, which was only to be expected. Oh, and there was one more condition as well: Mattaniah was to change his name to "Zedekiah".

Then Mattaniah was taken away again; he had one day to make his decision.

The next day, Mattaniah was brought back before the supreme commander and gave his answer: he agreed to all of the conditions set out by King Nebuchadnezzar.

I was told that it was quite a ceremony and that "Zedekiah" had given his hand in confirmation of the covenant and taken an oath in the name of Yahweh, the God of Israel.

Under those conditions, King Nebuchadnezzar's oath, sworn in the names of his gods, came into effect. The king of Babylon would allow the kingdom of Judah to continue, and promised to protect it as necessary should any other nation seek retribution for Judah's cooperation with the king of Babylon.

God's prophecy about Jeconiah was to be fulfilled: he would go to Babylon and none of his sons would sit on the throne.

But contrary to my expectations, a new king would sit on the throne of David and rule in Jerusalem. I desperately hoped that Zedekiah would prove to be a better king than Jehoiakim or Jeconiah. Even at that stage, I still hoped that repentance was possible.

☙

Once Zedekiah had accepted Nebuchadnezzar's terms and confirmed his agreement with an oath, events moved swiftly.

Zedekiah was brought back into the city and my brother's services were demanded for the anointing of the new king. King Nebuchadnezzar could have dispensed with this formality, but the anointing showed that Zedekiah was a properly appointed king, supported by the ordinary political processes of Judah. This increased his legitimacy as king and made it more likely that his subjects would support him.

All of Jeconiah's family and household had been cleared out of the royal palace already – indeed, most of them were being made ready to undertake the long and uncomfortable trek to Babylon.

Now, Zedekiah was installed in the palace with his family, and new servants and advisors were chosen. Nebuchadnezzar's representatives would remain in the palace with King Zedekiah for the foreseeable future too, making sure that the young man fully understood what was required of him as part of the growing Babylonian Empire.

Zedekiah was told firmly and clearly that Nebuchadnezzar did not ever want to have to visit Jerusalem in anger again. Judah must be a trustworthy vassal kingdom that would maintain a peaceful border with Egypt – until Nebuchadnezzar had the time and resources to turn his attention to taking over Egypt as well.

As the shackling of the captives continued, Nebuchadnezzar's army prepared to depart. The catapults and other machines of war were disassembled and loaded on wagons. The siege walls that surrounded the city were broken down and the roads leading into Jerusalem were cleared.

We who remained in the city were not allowed to leave the city at all while the prisoners were being processed – unless we were put to work delivering the booty to the camp. Maybe I looked a little too old for carrying heavy loads, so I stayed in the city throughout those weeks.

Eventually, though, the shackling of the exiles was finished, and the supreme commander led the army away. Many thousands of exiles followed at the rear, forming long, dispirited lines, carrying their heavy chains as best they could. Supervisors with whips walked nearby, ready to encourage them as necessary.

Once again, I stood watching on the wall as the long lines of men, women and children began their hopeless walk that would last many months. Scores of them would never reach Babylon, as exhaustion and disease took their toll and rendered the journey impossible. I was too far away to see clearly the expressions on the faces of the exiles, but there was no doubt that the heads of most were turned towards Jerusalem and the homes they would never see again. Reluctantly, they marched north into the unknown.

Hanamel my cousin and Gemariah my brother were both with me on the wall, and we turned and looked at each other as the last of the exiles disappeared from view over the hill.

"What now, Jeremiah?" Hanamel asked quietly. "What happens to our kingdom now?"

"I can't be sure. Yes, God gives me prophecies to deliver, but most of the time he doesn't explain in detail what they mean. I don't know when they will be fulfilled. Jeconiah and his mother have gone into exile along with all of his family, and that is just as God said it would be. Yet Jerusalem has not been destroyed, although I have not seen any great repentance. As a result, I assume that God's prophecies of destruction will be fulfilled at some time in the future, but I don't know when. Will it be soon? I don't think that I can be sure."

"Being a prophet doesn't seem to help much with understanding what God's prophecies mean, does it?" asked Hanamel.

"No, I'm afraid not," I agreed.

"If you, who are supposedly a prophet of God, cannot be sure what is going on, how can we poor ignorant priests know what to believe about these words that you say are from God?" Gemariah spoke sarcastically, but I couldn't help thinking that there was some truth in what he said.

"Well, there is no doubt about these words being from God," I replied, "but I do not have the understanding God has. As I have done several times before, I will reconsider all of God's prophecies and see if these latest events make any of the other prophecies any clearer." I spoke slowly. Life as a prophet had always been difficult for me, and it didn't seem to be getting any easier. It was good to see some prophecies being fulfilled so clearly, but that merely seemed to highlight my lack of comprehension of many of the others. When and how would they be fulfilled?

"So the total destruction you keep going on about isn't happening yet?" Gemariah's words sounded harsh, but I don't think he intended them that way. He was just finding it hard to understand why a prophet with heavy tidings about the future would not know how they would be fulfilled.

⳩

We were now free to come and go, although there were still many Chaldean soldiers monitoring everything that happened in the city, while other units of their army were still spread through the country, so that we quickly learned to keep off the highways to avoid them.

Hanamel and I walked to Anathoth one afternoon to see what had happened there during the siege. We knew that the Chaldean army had moved freely through the land during that time, as there had been no organised resistance outside Jerusalem.

We found the town still busy with people, although they were quick to point out that quite a few of the inhabitants had fallen foul of the Chaldean soldiers and been killed. My ancestral home had obviously been occupied by soldiers for some time, and I concluded that it would take a considerable amount of work and expense to restore it to its previous condition. The door at the front of the house was no longer the well-fitted door I remembered – instead, it hung crookedly and would not close properly. Inside, cooking implements were scattered across the main room, and many of our goods were spread carelessly around – seeming much the worse for wear. Bedding was strewn throughout the various rooms and expensive clothing seemed to have been used for wiping out pots and pans.

The happiest discovery I made was that the scroll room had been left largely untouched. Many scrolls had been emptied from the shelves and cupboards and lay piled in one corner, but there were no obvious signs of wanton destruction. After suffering the loss of several friends to death and exile, this was a joy that I had not expected.

Hanamel reported that the damage in our house was fairly typical of that in many houses around Anathoth, particularly houses that had not been occupied when the Chaldeans arrived.

In the middle of the afternoon, I left the town to return to Jerusalem. As Hanamel stayed to help clean up his father's house, I was alone when I crested the ridge and saw Jerusalem spread out below me.

From that distance, it seemed almost as if nothing had changed, yet below me lay a city from which most of the people had gone. Death and exile had stolen Jerusalem's population. The city that had been so full of people was left quiet and largely empty.

I looked down on the city and wondered what would happen next. How did God view Jerusalem now? Had he kept in the city those whom he wanted to bless? Had he sent away or killed those who deserved punishment? I considered the people who had been taken away and it didn't seem to fit very well, but how could I know?

As I stood there, with the afternoon sun shining warmly on the temple, still with its two massive bronze columns in front, I gradually seemed to be able to see the front of the temple more clearly than I would expect. It is hard to describe, but as I watched, I seemed to be able to see details as closely as if I were inside the temple courts themselves. It was an amazing feeling, and as it strengthened, the familiar feeling of a smouldering fire began. It expanded, slowly at first, but then swiftly, until there was no question that this was the work of Yahweh.

As I watched, the Lord showed me a vision: two baskets of figs standing before the temple of the Lord. One basket had very good figs, like first-ripe figs, but the other basket had very bad figs, so bad that they could not be eaten. God asked me,

"What do you see, Jeremiah?"[42]

"Figs," I replied, "the good figs very good, and the bad figs very bad, so bad that they cannot be eaten."

"Thus says the Lord, the God of Israel:
Like these good figs, so I will regard as good
the exiles from Judah, whom I have sent away
from this place to the land of the Chaldeans.
I will set my eyes on them for good,
and I will bring them back to this land.
I will build them up, and not tear them down;
I will plant them, and not pluck them up.
I will give them a heart to know that I am the Lord,
and they shall be my people and I will be their God,
for they shall return to me with their whole heart.

"But thus says the Lord:
Like the bad figs that are so bad they cannot be eaten,
so will I treat Zedekiah the king of Judah, his officials,
the remnant of Jerusalem who remain in this land,

---

[42] Jeremiah 24:3

and those who dwell in the land of Egypt.
I will make them a horror
to all the kingdoms of the earth,
to be a reproach, a byword, a taunt, and a curse
in all the places where I shall drive them.
And I will send sword, famine,
and pestilence upon them,
until they shall be utterly destroyed
from the land that I gave to them and their fathers."[43]

Then the vision faded and my eyes could again see the temple as it was, a distant and mostly deserted building, crowning a city that showed the ravages of a three-month siege. Thousands of people had gone, and how that would change the city was yet to be seen.

I had wondered what God thought of those who remained in the city, and now I knew. They were like rotten fruit – and I must stay as part of them. God's work for me was not yet finished.

---

[43] Jeremiah 24:5-10

Chapter 9

A letter

Just after the Chaldean army left, I saw a common thing that disgusted me but also filled me with anger: many of the people who had not been taken into captivity were offering sacrifices to their idols to thank them for their salvation!

Now, how could anyone justify that? It was Yahweh alone who had prophesied judgement and destruction, while all the false prophets had prophesied the nice things that everyone wanted to hear. Yet once God's prophecies came true, those who were spared exile thanked the so-called gods that had got nothing right!

One frustrating thing that I have learned through life is that people never believe anything they don't want to believe – however obvious the facts may be.

God had spoken of the people who remained in the city as "bad figs", and I began to wonder whether the people who remained in the city were indeed the worst parts of the audience I had been speaking to so fruitlessly for the last thirty years. I clearly recall asking myself whether the problems that had come from working as a prophet over those decades were about to get even worse.

I tried reminding people of the words of Yahweh: his predictions about the invasion by the king of Babylon, the death of Jehoiakim and the exile of Jeconiah. As often as I could, I reminded both individuals and crowds of the reasons God had given for his judgements, but crowds were hard to find, and few individuals would listen at all.

Sadly, my brother Azariah was far from pleased to hear my message. He wanted to present a message of patience and tolerance, of a God who would forgive, and most certainly would never punish his people – a sort of gentle and undemanding rich uncle who constantly gave and never demanded anything in return.

He saw me as a divisive figure: blaming idol worshippers for the trouble that had come upon Jerusalem, and threatening worse trouble if people would not repent. I certainly was blaming idolatry for our troubles, but why should that be seen as divisive? A united repentance was the best possible solution – in fact, the only positive solution – to our situation. Division or conflict would arise only if people refused to take this obvious step – and how was it my fault if people did that?

Yahweh was right; idols were wrong. Yahweh could tell the future; idols could do nothing. Their so-called prophets told everyone exactly what they wanted to hear, then when they were proved wrong, made excuses and provided a new collection of warm-sounding words of wishful thinking.

Some of my hearers had listened to enough of my prophecies in the past to think that they could win the argument by reminding me that I had said that Nebuchadnezzar would destroy the city and the temple, and had been completely wrong. I reminded them soberly that Nebuchadnezzar was not dead yet. Nothing was stopping him from coming back and finishing the job he had begun.

Nevertheless, the idolaters did not like my words; nor did my brother Azariah. One day he called me in to see him in the High Priest's house. After he had told me his grievance, I reminded him of the words in the Book of the Law of Yahweh which Josiah had read to the people back in the days when our father had been the High Priest:

> "You know how we lived in the land of Egypt, and how we came through the midst of the nations through which you passed. And you have seen their detestable things, their idols of wood and stone, of silver and gold, which were among them. Beware lest there be among you a man or woman or clan or tribe whose heart is turning away today from the Lord our God to go and serve the gods of those nations. Beware lest there be among you a root bearing poisonous and bitter fruit, one who, when he hears the words of this sworn covenant, blesses himself in his heart, saying, 'I shall be safe, though I walk in the stubbornness of my heart.' This will lead to the sweeping away of moist and dry alike. The Lord will not be willing to forgive him, but rather the anger of the Lord and his jealousy will smoke against that man, and the curses written in this book will settle upon him, and the Lord will blot out his name from under heaven. And the Lord will single him out from all the tribes of Israel for calamity, in accordance with all the curses of the covenant written in this Book of the Law."[44]

Maybe if I had had a younger brother I would have understood better why Azariah never liked me reminding

---

[44] Deuteronomy 29:16-21

him – the High Priest! – of the words of Yahweh. I do know that there was no easier way to get him annoyed than to point out to him the words of Yahweh, the God he was meant to represent to the people. To be honest, he really did have a good knowledge of God's words, but there were many he didn't want to apply if he could think of any other passage that could provide even the slightest hint of support for his preferred way of thinking.

One of his favourite descriptions of God was when Yahweh described himself to Moses; but he only used part of it. The rest he ignored. The part he liked said:

> "The Lord, the Lord, a God merciful and gracious, slow to anger, and abounding in steadfast love and faithfulness, keeping steadfast love for thousands, forgiving iniquity and transgression and sin,…"[45]

However, he always stopped short before he reached the words:

> "…but who will by no means clear the guilty, visiting the iniquity of the fathers on the children and the children's children, to the third and the fourth generation."[46]

Not only that, but he completely ignored the section just a few sentences later when Yahweh said:

> "You shall tear down their altars and break their pillars and cut down their Asherim (for you shall worship no other god, for the Lord, whose name is Jealous, is a jealous God)."[47]

On that day, in his annoyance, he started to quote me the first part, but stopped in confusion as he saw the gleam in my eye which warned him that I would probably finish

---

[45] Exodus 34:6-7a

[46] Exodus 34:7b

[47] Exodus 34:13-14

his quote for him if he went that far! The word of God should only be used honestly, not in attempts to twist it to our own purposes.

It was yet another source of anger between us.

I feel now that it was after this interview that I first sensed my brother's feelings towards me passing from anger and irritation to outright hatred.

$$\text{\LARGE \ss}$$

For a little while, Jerusalem was quite empty. Houses stood with their doors wide open, and no owner came to close them. For a very short time, no one seemed to know quite what to do, but opportunities bring opportunists. Soon people were investigating the empty houses everywhere and seeing if the soldiers had left behind anything of value. Treasure hunters searched the empty houses of the exiled rich, hunting for hidden valuables.

Nothing was sure. Law was never certain. Strength was all that mattered, and some of the poor who were not averse to violence increased their wealth quickly.

Over this city of disorder and mayhem, the new king, Zedekiah, must learn to preside; but he had no time for preparation or training. Nebuchadnezzar's representatives gave advice, but their recommendations were harsh, demanding a leader with resolution and a conviction that the end justified the means. Zedekiah showed very quickly that he was neither a leader nor a man of resolution. He wanted to please everyone, and he was not a harsh young man. Even among his friends, he was not a leader, yet now the responsibility for an entire nation lay on his shoulders.

Within days, relatives and opportunists from all over Judah were arriving in Jerusalem to claim the empty houses and sundry goods. There was at least one claimant for every empty house, although many seemed to know surprisingly little about the "close relative" they were professing such devotion for. However, many genuinely concerned citizens did come to Jerusalem to enquire about the health of their beloved relatives from whom the siege and subsequent mayhem had separated them. They came in hope of finding their relatives safe, and happy reunions rewarded the care of some.

I once saw two middle-aged women suddenly squeal and run towards each other on a quiet street. It was a greeting that was full of joy, but only for a few moments. Their discussions quickly left them in tears as they heard news of other family members and close friends who had died in Jerusalem and in a little town down in the south of Judah. Nebuchadnezzar's army had passed through both places, leaving much damage and many dead.

On another occasion, I saw a man and a woman knocking on the door of a house near that of the High Priest. It had been the home of a rich old man who I knew had been taken into exile by the Chaldeans. The house had already been claimed by a man who was short and fat – and convincingly rich. He came from a village near Jerusalem, he said, and he claimed that the old man was his next of kin – an uncle with neither wife nor children. There was nobody in any of the houses nearby – they had all been taken to Babylon – and nobody seemed able to either confirm or contradict the claimant's story. Nobody, that is, until I watched this couple arrive. They did what they could to get the attention of anyone inside the house, and eventually the new occupant came to the door, opening it slowly and peering around the door in a suspicious way.

"You!" said the man and his wife together, then the man continued angrily, "What are you doing here?"

"I am staying in my uncle's house, as I have a perfect right to do," responded the claimant, smoothly.

" 'A perfect right!' You said you were never going anywhere near him again, and he told you he didn't want you to."

Gradually the details of the story came out, and it became clear that the claimant was who he claimed to be, but only up to a point. The couple with whom he was now arguing were actually the son and daughter-in-law of the old man who owned the house. The case was referred to the judges and would be settled at some time in the future, but in the meantime, the claimant would justly be evicted from the house. One of the difficulties was that the old owner might well not survive the journey to Babylon – his age was against him. But it would probably be some considerable time before any news would be received about the journey and any casualties along the way. News would not be very common.

The judges were kept busy for many months making decisions about who would be given control of the houses so ruthlessly emptied by the Chaldeans. Gradually, the city filled up again. Some of the judges were more open than others to the convincing effects of money, and various rich people took control of many houses that should probably have been the property of various poorer people.

The temple began to fill again too. Some more priests came from the towns in the areas of Judah and Benjamin, but it was clear that there would not be enough for the work, particularly at feast times. To be sure, the feasts were not kept as Josiah had wanted them kept, but there were still quite a few who came and needed the help of a priest.

I had become accustomed to the idea that I would never work as a priest again, but the urgent shortage made even me desirable as a priest! Azariah asked me if I could work as a priest whenever the round of feasts caused a critical shortage of priests. I wasn't sure how long the arrangement would last, but I agreed anyway.

At the same time, there were also quite a few houses for sale in Jerusalem – mostly being sold by relatives who had inherited houses from people who had died in the siege or its aftermath, but who had no wish to live in Jerusalem themselves. Prices were lower than usual because of the lack of demand, and I took the opportunity to buy a small house quite near the temple. It was good to be able to stop imposing on Hanamel's hospitality and to have a place of my own to live in.

I told my mother that she was welcome to live with me if she wanted to. My work as a prophet to the nations had taken me away from Judah so much after my father's death that I had not been able to look after her as much as I would have liked. Although my brothers had cared for her well through those years, I hoped that I would finally be able to look after her as a son should.

By that time, she was 75 years old – an old woman, really, despite the wonderful health she still enjoyed. She had been a widow for more than twenty years by then, and I found being with her a great encouragement. We still revelled in any time we could spend together discussing God's word and his ways.

ℛ

Nebuchadnezzar's officers still remained in Judah, carefully scrutinising all of Zedekiah's decisions. Only those that were approved were ever communicated to the people. The officers were really Zedekiah's supervisors, and they were hard-faced, unemotional men who showed little sympathy for anybody.

They refused to get involved in any religious matters, and no rules about religious behaviour were promulgated during their tenure in the capital. Of course, that didn't mean that there was no religious input from anyone. God's words were still there for me to deliver, and his condemnations and warnings were just as clear as they had been when God first gave them to me in Josiah's time. I delivered them, but I was badly outnumbered: many false prophets and idolatrous priests were promoting messages of immorality, lust and vice, and their messages were much more popular than mine.

Nebuchadnezzar had obviously had some misgivings about Zedekiah's leadership, because he had required Zedekiah to report periodically. Presumably Nebuchadnezzar's officers had to report too, and no doubt Nebuchadnezzar compared the reports and drew his own conclusions.

Zedekiah's first report was due to be sent six months after Nebuchadnezzar's army had left with the hapless Jewish captives, and I heard about it only because my brother Gemariah was given the job of taking the report to Babylon. Our family had been important in Judah for centuries, so it was not really surprising that he was chosen to take the letter and represent Zedekiah before King Nebuchadnezzar. Nevertheless, it was a great honour and responsibility for him, and he would be away for several months, along with Elasah the son of Shaphan, who had also been selected for the important task. It was an important honour for Elasah also.

Surprisingly, none of Ahikam's family had been punished for the misstep which had occasioned his summary execution. Both his brother Elasah and his nephew Gedaliah had been included in Zedekiah's staff, with Elasah working in the palace as an advisor, and Gedaliah in an important position within the civil administration of Jerusalem.

I heard the unexpected news from Gemariah just two days before he was to leave with Elasah on their long journey to Babylon. I had never visited Babylon myself, and I think that Gemariah was rather pleased at that. He was the middle son, sandwiched between the High Priest and a notorious prophet, and was often overlooked when people were looking for someone to do an important task.

It was mid-afternoon when I heard the news, and as soon as I arrived back home, I felt the irresistible presence of God and heard his words of command. Word by word, his instructions were seared into my mind. I was to write a letter and send it with Elasah and Gemariah. The exiles might be out of sight, but they were not out of the mind of our God who had sent them away from their land.

The letter must be written quickly, but it would be best to enlist Baruch's help if possible. My messy writing would not make it easy for the recipients to read this important message!

As usual, I felt the urge to act as soon as the presence of God had left me. Straight away, I went in search of Baruch, glad that he had been not been taken away into captivity. I needed him.

Very quickly, I found him in his chamber in the temple.

"Baruch," I said, a little breathless after being touched by God's hand and then having hurried into the temple. "I need you to write an urgent letter for me!"

"The Lord bless you, Jeremiah," replied Baruch, gently chiding me for having skipped the customary formalities of greeting in my haste.

"The Lord keep you," I responded hurriedly. "I have to send a letter to the exiles in Babylon. Straight away."

"Why the desperate urgency, Jeremiah?"

"Elasah and Gemariah are leaving for Babylon very early in the morning, just the day after tomorrow."

"Is it a long letter?" Baruch asked doubtfully. He had written some very long documents for me before, and there was no way that he could have written anything that long in the time available. I was glad to be able to reassure him that this letter was not very long.

"Ah, good," he smiled at me, relieved. "I am busy working on a deed for a house down near the Potsherd Gate. The old owner was killed by a missile from one of the Chaldean catapults and the new owner wants to sell it. He was referred to me as one of the best scribes to produce such a deed of sale. Have a look at it." I looked politely at the sheet he showed me, and it certainly showed a scribe's work at its best. "It looks beautiful, doesn't it?" he continued. "If only there were better things than bills of sale to challenge my skill. Never mind. Items like this will continue to build my reputation as a scribe, and it pays the bills too."

"Baruch, I need this letter to be written on parchment," I said. "It will be directed to all of the exiles in Babylon, so it needs to be made to last, and parchment is best for that."

"Yes, parchment it will be, and I can do it for you right now," said Baruch, rubbing his hands. I knew that he far preferred to work with parchment, as it normally lasts much longer than papyrus, and everyone wants to produce work that will last.

Parchment is not cheap, but there was not much point in writing a letter that would fall apart before everyone for whom it was written had had a chance to read it. Although I knew little about where the exiles had been sent, it seemed likely that they would be in several different places, and that the letter would have to be read by many different people.

"Very well, Jeremiah. How long is your letter?"

"I haven't counted the words exactly, but I'm fairly sure there will only be about 300 to 400 words."

Baruch put aside the deed that he was working on and looked through the selection of sheets of parchment that sat on one side of his desk.

"I'll just get the right ink too," he said, standing up and walking over to a shelf on the wall. He reached past a few larger containers and selected a small ink well. He shook it gently, then opened it and smelled it carefully. Satisfied, he returned to his desk and sat down, placing the ink well within easy reach.

"I'm ready," he said, and we began.

I stood behind Baruch, reading the words of God from within my mind, speaking each word clearly and carefully. After I had read a sentence, I noticed that Baruch was not writing, but looking at me thoughtfully instead, and I suddenly realised that I was not speaking in my ordinary voice, but in an imitation of the voice that God seems to use when I hear him in my mind.

The letter Baruch wrote read like this:

"Thus says the Lord of hosts, the God of Israel,
to all the exiles whom I have sent into exile
from Jerusalem to Babylon:
Build houses and live in them;
plant gardens and eat their produce.
Take wives and have sons and daughters;
take wives for your sons,
and give your daughters in marriage,
that they may bear sons and daughters;
multiply there, and do not decrease.
But seek the welfare of the city
where I have sent you into exile,
and pray to the Lord on its behalf,
for in its welfare you will find your welfare.
For thus says the Lord of hosts, the God of Israel:
Do not let your prophets and your diviners
who are among you deceive you,

and do not listen to the dreams that they dream,
for it is a lie that they are prophesying
to you in my name;
I did not send them,
declares the Lord.

"For thus says the Lord:
When seventy years are completed for Babylon,
I will visit you, and I will fulfil to you my promise
and bring you back to this place.
For I know the plans I have for you, declares the Lord,
plans for welfare and not for evil,
to give you a future and a hope.
Then you will call upon me and come and pray to me,
and I will hear you. You will seek me and find me,
when you seek me with all your heart.
I will be found by you, declares the Lord,
and I will restore your fortunes
and gather you from all the nations
and all the places where I have driven you,
declares the Lord, and I will bring you back to the place
from which I sent you into exile."[48]

Baruch is a careful but speedy scribe, and in well under an hour the letter was complete, each character carefully etched in a clear black ink that would make reading a pleasure. Once the ink was dry, he handed me the sheet and I read the letter carefully. This was the word of God, so I must make sure that it was written without errors. It was no surprise when I found no errors at all: Baruch really did have a remarkable skill, and a simple letter like this didn't really test him very much. I imagined what the letter would have looked like if I had written it in my untidy scribble, and was thankful that others had skills which I lacked.

---

[48] Jeremiah 29:4-14

I thanked Baruch for his work, paid him his scribe's fee and took the sheet, rolling it up and tying it with string to keep it in good condition throughout the long journey.

Next, I found Gemariah again and asked him to take the letter with him and deliver it to the exiles in Babylon.

"I'm sorry, but I can't even tell you exactly who to give it to," I said. "I'm not sure who amongst the elders will have survived the arduous journey."

"Is this another diatribe, Jeremiah?" asked Gemariah, doubtfully. "Are you making things even worse for the exiles when they already have enough trouble?"

"I don't think so," I replied. "It seems to be a message of kindness and generosity from God. Would you like to hear it?"

Gemariah inclined his head in agreement, so I recited the words of the letter to him.

"Seventy years?" he asked in blank amazement, seeming shocked at the length of the punishment, no doubt thinking of the generations lost in a foreign land. "Seventy years in exile?"

"Yes," I replied, "seventy years. Don't you remember that God had already said that? It must have been about seven or eight years ago, just around the time when the first group of our people went into captivity in the fourth year of Jehoiakim."

"Did he?" Gemariah responded absently. "I don't remember. It can't have made much of an impression on me. Maybe it was because there weren't so many people taken that time."

"Or maybe because you didn't believe it was the word of God," I responded, a little irritably.

"Jeremiah, just put yourself in my position," said Gemariah, looking at me apologetically. "How could I believe you when it has taken so long for anything to happen? And no-one else has believed you, either."

❧

Early in the morning of the next day, Gemariah and Elasah left, accompanied by a troop of armed men and carrying Zedekiah's sealed report for Nebuchadnezzar. God's precious letter went with them also.

Chapter 10

Joy and judgement

I saw a host of people. They started from towns and cities throughout Babylon and Assyria, from Persia and Media. Eagerness was in all their faces as they closed the doors of their erstwhile houses and walked away, without looking back. Individuals and families met and formed small groups. Group met group and the greetings were full of purpose. Like rivulets meeting and merging, they formed larger groups and the eagerness grew. Quiet determination gradually became a more obvious intent; spoken of, planned. Roads that led to Israel were the riverbeds that guided, first a trickle, but then a growing flood of people returning to the promised land.

> "…fear not, O Jacob my servant, declares the Lord,
> nor be dismayed, O Israel;
> for behold, I will save you from far away,
> and your offspring from the land of their captivity.
> Jacob shall return and have quiet and ease,
> and none shall make him afraid.

For I am with you to save you, declares the Lord."[49]

I saw them as they arrived at the borders of Israel. With the unquestioning knowledge that always permeates a dream, I felt their gladness at their return to the land of our fathers. I shared their sorrow too, at the blackened ruins that met their eyes, the cities scraped from the tops of hills and piled as rubble in the valleys, while the hills had become wooded heights. I watched as the earliest of them caught their first glimpse of Jerusalem, now fire-blackened and strewn with fallen masonry. The valley of the Kidron was filled with the rubbish of utter destruction, and I saw their courage falter as the size of the task, the enormity of their duty, struck home.

"Thus says the Lord:
Behold, I will restore the fortunes of the tents of Jacob
and have compassion on his dwellings;
the city shall be rebuilt on its mound,
and the palace shall stand where it used to be."[50]

I watched as their courage rebounded and every man's hand worked with the hand of his neighbour to build and to rebuild. Houses and walls were built once more, and the temple and palace grew swiftly out of the piles of rubble. Through every act of construction, the determination of the returned exiles grew stronger: with God's help, they would overcome.

Again I saw a host of people, wending their way along many different paths to Jerusalem. Young and old together, the women and children not left behind. I heard their mingled songs of praise and the joy that filled the air as the rebuilt walls of Jerusalem came in sight. I felt the blessedness and worship as the temple of Yahweh was filled with his glory.

---

[49] Jeremiah 30:10-11
[50] Jeremiah 30:18

"Out of them shall come songs of thanksgiving,
and the voices of those who celebrate.
I will multiply them, and they shall not be few;
I will make them honoured, and they shall not be small.
Their children shall be as they were of old,
and their congregation shall be established before me,
and I will punish all who oppress them.
Their prince shall be one of themselves;
their ruler shall come out from their midst;
I will make him draw near, and he shall approach me,
for who would dare of himself to approach me?
declares the Lord.
And you shall be my people, and I will be your God."[51]

The temple was crowded with happy, praising throngs. No longer was the worship of God a burden, nor did worry for the future keep any from praising Yahweh on this joyous occasion.

"They shall come and sing aloud on the height of Zion,
and they shall be radiant over the goodness of the Lord,
over the grain, the wine, and the oil,
and over the young of the flock and the herd;
their life shall be like a watered garden,
and they shall languish no more.
Then shall the young women rejoice in the dance,
and the young men and the old shall be merry.
I will turn their mourning into joy;
I will comfort them, and give them gladness for sorrow.
I will feast the soul of the priests with abundance,
and my people shall be satisfied with my goodness,
declares the Lord."[52]

Intermingled with the praise were threads of sadness and guilt: an acknowledgement of past sins and a deep thankfulness for the undeserved favour of a loving,

---

[51] Jeremiah 30:19-22
[52] Jeremiah 31:12-14

forgiving God. I woke and my sleep had been pleasant.[53] The oft-repeated nightmares so common in my life as a prophet had relaxed their grip for one night at least.

I lay on my bed and revelled in the feeling of joy and happiness, the sheer pleasure of seeing the worship of God springing freely from the heart of my people. I knew the vision must speak of a time in the future, presumably after the 70 years of captivity that had now already begun – at least for some. My own short life would end well before that time, but how glad I was to know that it would come to pass!

For quite some time, the ecstasy of the vision I had been experiencing filled me with positive thoughts. Yet after a while, I began to wonder how things would continue after that first flush of enthusiasm. Would the re-gathering establish Israel and Judah as a single kingdom again, and if so, how long would it be before disunity and discontentment broke out again among my people?

Yet as I lay and wondered, I felt a sense of peace enveloping me again as God soothed my fears, calming me. Though I remained awake, I began to see again the land as I had seen it in my dream, as if I was seeing the story continue.

As I watched, the land again filled with people. Babies were born and given names that honoured Yahweh. Sheep and cattle grazed in the fields throughout the land, yet the wild animals left them in peace.

"Behold, the days are coming, declares the Lord,
when I will sow the house of Israel
and the house of Judah
with the seed of man and the seed of beast.
And it shall come to pass that

---

[53] Jeremiah 31:26

> as I have watched over them
> to pluck up and break down,
> to overthrow, destroy, and bring harm,
> so I will watch over them to build and to plant,
> declares the Lord."[54]

Pervading God's message was the feeling that the past was past, and that never again would unfaithfulness and godlessness take God's chosen people away from his love.

> "For this is the covenant that I will make
> with the house of Israel after those days,
> declares the Lord:
> I will put my law within them,
> and I will write it on their hearts.
> And I will be their God, and they shall be my people.
> And no longer shall each one teach his neighbour
> and each his brother, saying, 'Know the Lord,'
> for they shall all know me,
> from the least of them to the greatest,
> declares the Lord.
> For I will forgive their iniquity,
> and I will remember their sin no more."[55]

That night may have been the happiest time in all my communing with God. It was a time of peace and tranquillity; of hope and expectation.

CR

Five months after I had sent God's letter with Gemariah and Elasah to Babylon, they returned to Jerusalem. The journey had been long and tiring, but there had been little apparent danger.

During their absence, no important messages seemed to have come to Jerusalem from Babylon, so I had

---

[54] Jeremiah 31:27-28
[55] Jeremiah 31:33-34

assumed that Nebuchadnezzar must have been reasonably content with the report from Zedekiah. Certainly nothing obvious seemed to change in the governing of the kingdom.

However, I had been a little concerned since sending the letter, wondering how the exiles would respond to its message and whether it might be reported to the Chaldeans. I had no idea how they would react if the letter was shown to them.

Soon after Gemariah's return, I went to see him.

"The Lord bless you, Jeremiah," he greeted me. From the look on his face it was clear that he had much to tell.

"The Lord keep you," I responded, and we immediately began to speak of his journey to Babylon and of the wonders of the city itself. He had been utterly amazed by its grandeur. Its enormous gateways and huge buildings had taken his breath away, while its wide avenues and luxurious buildings had reminded him that this was the city that had become the centre of the world. Wealth was obvious on all sides. Statues, temples, gardens, processions and parties were everywhere, and Nebuchadnezzar's greatness was on full display.

The exiles from Judah had been distributed across several different regions of Babylonia and seemed to be settling in well. In fact, Gemariah described their general attitude as confident and self-assured. Although many of the exiles had to work hard on Nebuchadnezzar's building projects, they were not being oppressed as cruelly as our fathers had been in Egypt. It was as if the centre of Judah had been transplanted to Babylon. Religion was blossoming, and the gods of Babylon were being added to the wide range of gods that many of the exiles already worshipped. A pliable collection of prophets was giving messages the people wanted to hear, just as God's letter had warned – prophets who were apparently predicting that the exile would be over in only a year or two and that the exiles would soon be returning home.

Gemariah told me that he had passed on the letter I had sent and I eagerly asked him if he had been given any message or letter for me. But there had been no message. I was a little surprised to get no response to God's blunt words, but realised that maybe it was for the best. Possibly they were thinking carefully about God's words.

"You know, it was probably best that you stayed in Jerusalem, Jeremiah," Gemariah added. "You would probably have been beaten up – no-one liked your words. Seventy years is a long time."

Gemariah also named two of the leaders of the captives who had been particularly voluble: Ahab the son of Kolaiah and Zedekiah the son of Maaseiah. I took special note of the names of the troublemakers, thinking that they might be important. They were.

❧

A few days later, Zephaniah, the priest who was second to Azariah and looked after the administrative side of the priesthood, came to me with a letter. It was from Shemaiah, a man whom I knew slightly and considered a troublemaker. He was originally from Nehelam, a town about 15 kilometres[56] southwest of Jerusalem, but had moved to Jerusalem about a year before Nebuchadnezzar had invaded the land. He had been taken into exile with Jeconiah. Apparently the letter was addressed to all of the priests, but directed to Zephaniah rather than my brother. Possibly Shemaiah didn't want to upset my brother, since maybe he thought that Azariah would support me – in which case he was sadly misinformed, I'm sure.

---

[56] 10 miles.

Shemaiah probably assumed that Zephaniah would know that his letter was not intended to be shown to me, or maybe he forgot that I was a priest; either way, though, Zephaniah took the addressing literally, and read the letter to me. It said:

> "The Lord has made you priest instead of Jehoiada the priest, to have charge in the house of the Lord over every madman who prophesies, to put him in the stocks and neck irons. Now why have you not rebuked Jeremiah of Anathoth who is prophesying to you? For he has sent to us in Babylon, saying, 'Your exile will be long; build houses and live in them, and plant gardens and eat their produce.' "[57]

As I listened to the letter, I wasn't sure how to respond. Several possible responses chased each other through my mind, but I didn't know which would be best. However, when I asked Zephaniah to read it again, a hardness came into my mind as he did so, and it was instantly clear that God was not at all unsure what the best response was!

Yahweh's words filled me again, clear and bright. I could hear them, and could read them on the wall of my mind:

"Send to all the exiles, saying,
'Thus says the Lord concerning Shemaiah of Nehelam:
Because Shemaiah had prophesied to you
when I did not send him, and has made you trust in a lie,
therefore thus says the Lord: Behold, I will punish
Shemaiah of Nehelam and his descendants.
He shall not have anyone living among this people,
and he shall not see the good that I will do to my people,
declares the Lord,
for he has spoken rebellion against the Lord.' "[58]

---

[57] Jeremiah 29:26-28
[58] Jeremiah 29:30-32

God's voice stopped and, as usual, I felt driven to do something. Immediately. Another letter. I must find Baruch again and dictate this message too. I quickly thanked Zephaniah and began to usher him towards the door so that I could go to find Baruch, but as I did so, the voice of Yahweh began again, speaking this time to all the exiles:

"Because you have said,
'The Lord has raised up prophets
for us in Babylon,'
thus says the Lord
concerning the king who sits on the throne of David,
and concerning all the people who dwell in this city,
your kinsmen who did not go out with you into exile:
'Thus says the Lord of hosts, behold,
I am sending on them sword, famine, and pestilence,
and I will make them like vile figs
that are so rotten they cannot be eaten.
I will pursue them with sword, famine, and pestilence,
and will make them a horror
to all the kingdoms of the earth,
to be a curse, a terror, a hissing, and a reproach
among all the nations where I have driven them,
because they did not pay attention to my words,
declares the Lord,
that I persistently sent to you
by my servants the prophets,
but you would not listen,
declares the Lord.' "[59]

It seemed a little strange to be sending a message to exiles in Babylon about the heavy judgement that was coming on the people of Jerusalem – where I was living! Needless to say, there was also the uncomfortable feeling I always had when God condemned a group of which I was

---

[59] Jeremiah 29:15-19

part: was I excluded or not? However, I couldn't think about it for long, because God had more to say:

"Hear the word of the Lord, all you exiles
whom I sent away from Jerusalem to Babylon:
'Thus says the Lord of hosts, the God of Israel,
concerning Ahab the son of Kolaiah
and Zedekiah the son of Maaseiah,
who are prophesying a lie to you in my name:
Behold, I will deliver them into the hand
of Nebuchadnezzar king of Babylon,
and he shall strike them down before your eyes.
Because of them this curse shall be used
by all the exiles from Judah in Babylon:
"The Lord make you like Zedekiah and Ahab,
whom the king of Babylon roasted in the fire,"
because they have done an outrageous thing in Israel,
they have committed adultery
with their neighbours' wives,
and they have spoken in my name lying words
that I did not command them.
I am the one who knows, and I am witness,
declares the Lord.' "[60]

Hastily I found Baruch, and once again he used his God-given ability with a pen to write out God's words. Then this new letter was duly sent to the leaders of the exiles. Would they respond more positively this time? How long would it be before Ahab and Zedekiah were roasting in the fire?

CR

In all, Nebuchadnezzar's officers stayed in Judah for two full years through these events, and there was a collective sigh of relief when they finally left.

---

[60] Jeremiah 29:20-23

Over that time, Zedekiah had learned to satisfy the requirements of Nebuchadnezzar's men, but only now would it be revealed how he would behave once he was given free rein in the kingdom.

Chapter 11

Rebellion

As I said, there was a collective sigh of relief from the people when Nebuchadnezzar's officers finally left.

I wasn't quite sure how I felt about it.

Since Zedekiah's supervisors had refused to get involved in any religious matters or to allow Zedekiah to do so, nothing in Judah's worship had changed for the better during those two years. Instead, the worship of Yahweh had continued to go downhill – although I had not really believed that could be possible! At the time, I believed that Zedekiah would have liked to have encouraged better worship, but nothing was done – the king showed no leadership at all. Would things get better once Zedekiah had free rein in the kingdom?

Really, though, a "free rein" is probably not a very accurate description of how things were. King Zedekiah had promised to serve King Nebuchadnezzar, to pay the agreed tribute every year, and to faithfully obey any commands received from Babylon. Not only that, but he must present himself before Nebuchadnezzar every year to explain his actions over the preceding year.

To have honestly kept his side of the bargain, Zedekiah should have gone to Babylon before winter even began, a month or two before the end of the third year of his reign – but he stayed at home instead. The weather was cold and wet, and the royal advisors recommended against it. There was a growing feeling in Jerusalem that Zedekiah should show a little more "leadership", rather than just giving in to everything that Nebuchadnezzar demanded.

So, Zedekiah stayed at home through the winter. It was a risky step to take.

March, 594 BC – the 4th year of King Zedekiah

When the winter rains began to lessen and the growing warmth of spring announced the advent of a new year, Zedekiah left on the long trek to Babylon. With him went Baruch's younger brother Seraiah, who was Zedekiah's quartermaster. Most importantly from my point of view, Seraiah took with him another letter from Yahweh.

I had given Seraiah the letter, very conscious that I had strict instructions that must be followed, and hoping that I could pass on the importance of following them *exactly*.

Over time, God had given me various messages about Babylon, and during that winter he had added several more.

The great prophet Isaiah had spoken for God about a hundred years before me, and my familiarity with his writings had gradually taught me some of God's ways of working with his people. God's predictions are rarely given only once or twice. In fact, his warnings are frequently repeated several times over decades or even centuries, so that we can never say that he hasn't told us beforehand, or claim that important events have been orchestrated by idols.

Isaiah had been given several messages about Babylon too, and I re-read all of them often throughout that winter. They were prophecies that described the utter destruction of Babylon, well before it had ever become the important nation that it is today. God's prophecies sometimes seem puzzling because they speak of future events as the pre-existing foundation for events that will spring from them. Thus, Isaiah's words spoke of devastation coming to Babylon because of their cruelty in oppressing Israel, particularly the old people:

> "Sit in silence, and go into darkness,
> O daughter of the Chaldeans;
> for you shall no more be called
> the mistress of kingdoms.
> I was angry with my people;
> I profaned my heritage;
> I gave them into your hand;
> you showed them no mercy;
> on the aged you made your yoke
> exceedingly heavy."[61]

At that time, however, Babylon had been only a third-rate kingdom, answerable to the other, more important kingdoms that surrounded her. No mistress of kingdoms was Babylon at that time – not until Nebuchadnezzar had come to the fore.

Yet God had already spoken of her punishment through Isaiah:

> "The Lord has broken the staff of the wicked,

---

[61] Isaiah 47:5-6

the sceptre of rulers,
that struck the peoples in wrath
with unceasing blows,
that ruled the nations in anger
with unrelenting persecution."[62]

Yahweh's words to me about Babylon were very similar – and just as damning.

Then, about two weeks before Zedekiah set off, God gave me some detailed instructions about what I needed to do with these prophecies against Babylon. When I was younger, God had sent me to do many different things personally, giving me detailed instructions about how I should deliver his messages to many nations. In more recent times, though, he had directed me to arrange for others to complete the work: first sending a letter to Babylon with my brother Gemariah, and now performing this commission through Baruch's younger brother Seraiah.

I had visited many different lands, from Gaza to Elam, from Egypt to areas in the far north, but I had never seen Babylon, and it was beginning to appear that I never would. Instead, I seemed to be limited to the nations that would be attacked by Babylon. God's condemnation of the conqueror was to be delivered by others.

Baruch and Seraiah had pursued very different careers, but had maintained a close friendship throughout. By this time, Seraiah was a fairly senior officer in Zedekiah's army, being responsible for managing the stores and supplies of the entire army. Of course, there wasn't much of an army left, but it was still an important position, and I sometimes got the feeling that Baruch might be a little jealous of his younger brother's success. Seraiah was a competent officer and had been in the right place at the right time and had been

---

[62] Isaiah 14:5-6

appointed to the position by Zedekiah when the Chaldean officers left Judah. He was apparently a good, steady worker, just like his brother, although he lacked Baruch's artistic flair. Zedekiah had decided to take Seraiah with him to Babylon because he knew that Nebuchadnezzar would want detailed reports on the army and the situation at the southern border. Seraiah would be able to provide these details without removing an active leader from the units stationed at the border.

I discussed God's requirements briefly with Baruch, who in turn sounded out Seraiah. When Seraiah indicated that he may be able to do what I was asking, Baruch arranged a meeting between us. Unfortunately, though, Baruch was very busy, so I would have to write God's word myself this time.

The meeting was arranged for a day just one week before Zedekiah planned to leave, and in Baruch's house rather than my own. It was not that Zedekiah was specifically against me, but I felt that it would be better for Seraiah if it were not known that *I* had given him a scroll to carry to Babylon.

I was ready and waiting when Baruch ushered Seraiah into the main room of his house.

"Here is Jeremiah, the prophet," Baruch said to his brother, then, turning to me, he added, "and this is Seraiah, my brother – King Zedekiah's quartermaster." This last was said with some pride – in that strange, mixed-up way that envy affects us. Despite seeming to feel that Seraiah had been given a position of more importance than he deserved, Baruch was obviously proud of that position.

"The Lord be with you, Seraiah," I responded.

"The Lord bless you," answered Seraiah.

I was a few years older than Baruch and he in turn was a few years older than Seraiah, and that seniority made me responsible for leading the conversation. Besides, God's instructions had been quite detailed, so I had to make sure that they were all spelled out very clearly to Seraiah.

"Yahweh has spoken many words against the empire of Babylon," I began. "Now he wants those words announced in the capital of the empire itself."

"What do you mean, 'announced'?" asked Seraiah, quickly. "If you are wanting me to be a prophet like you, then forget it. I'm not that type of person."

"What God has commanded is that the words in the scroll that I will give you be read out loud – all of them – as you stand next to the Euphrates River. Don't worry, you won't have to read them in the main square of the city or say them to King Nebuchadnezzar or anything like that. But you will have to read them out loud and then add some extra words that I have written in a separate scroll."

"Well, that doesn't sound too difficult," replied Seraiah, slowly, sounding a little less apprehensive. "Is that all?"

"There are just a few more details that we need to get right," I answered, and Seraiah immediately looked more dubious again.

"Don't be so worried about it," Baruch reassured him. "God will look after you anyway."

"Hmm," said Seraiah, doubtfully, looking from me to Baruch and then back again with a long, searching look. "Announcing the future destruction of a nation in its own capital through the mouth of an army officer of a subjugated nation doesn't sound very safe to me."

"Haven't you heard the reports of what Nebuchadnezzar himself has said about Yahweh?" I asked. A few years before, we had heard reports through Zaccai and Abigail about a dream that Nebuchadnezzar had had. Through Daniel, God had interpreted the dream, and Nebuchadnezzar had acknowledged God's power. "Nebuchadnezzar announced that Yahweh is 'God of gods and Lord of kings, and a revealer of mysteries.' "[63]

"Yes, I heard about that, but I also heard what he did a few years later when three Jews wouldn't serve his gods. Didn't he have them thrown into a furnace? He's not a patient man, Jeremiah."

"You're right," I agreed, "they were thrown into his furnace, but God kept them safe, and in the end, Nebuchadnezzar had to admit again that Yahweh is great. That time he said that no-one was allowed to say anything against Yahweh or they would be torn apart and their house reduced to rubble."

"Oh, I didn't hear that part," admitted Seraiah.

"It all happened. Yahweh is still working – even today; even in Babylon."

"Alright, what else do I need to do?"

"When you finish saying the extra words in the second scroll that I will give you – you'll need to learn those – tie a stone to the first scroll and throw it into the river, the Euphrates. As it sinks," I explained, "you must say, 'Thus shall Babylon sink, to rise no more, because of the disaster that I am bringing upon her, and they shall become exhausted.'[64] That's all you need to do, but you must do it exactly."

"I think I can do that for you," said Seraiah.

"It's not for me, Seraiah, it's for Yahweh our God."

---

[63] Daniel 2:47
[64] Jeremiah 51:64

"I think I would prefer to do it for you. Yahweh is a hard taskmaster, it seems to me. Look at what has happened to our nation."

I paused for a while and thought about what he had said. I suppose that it could be reasonable to see God as a hard taskmaster if you look only at the end of the matter, when his patience has been exhausted. But what a misleading picture that gives! "God only becomes a hard taskmaster when we ignore his love," I replied, "ignore his patience and generosity, ignore the prophets he has sent to warn us. Ignore everything about him, until we blame him for our suffering when he finally punishes us."

"Anyway, can I see the scrolls I have to read out?"

I handed him the scroll with all of God's words against Babylon. He took it and unrolled it, scanning the columns of untidy writing. I could see that he was having difficulty reading some of the words, so I added, "You'll have to go over it a few times to make sure you can read it. My writing is not as good as your brother's."

"You're right," he agreed absently, and then looked a little uncomfortable as he realised what he had said. He looked at me apologetically and I smiled back reassuringly, thinking that it would probably be good for him to read the words a few times anyway. Seraiah was one of the few in Judah who still believed in Yahweh, and he was really quite dedicated in his worship. However, he acted as if religion had its proper place and should be kept clearly within those bounds. It seemed that his job as quartermaster would always be more important to him.

"When you come to Babylon, see that you read all the words in that scroll, and then say the words in this second scroll as well." I unrolled it and read it to him: " 'O Lord, you have said concerning this place that you will cut it off, so that nothing shall dwell in it, neither man nor beast, and it shall be desolate forever.' "[65] I rolled up the scroll again and handed it to him. "You will need to learn the words in that scroll," I reminded him, tapping the scroll as he held it, "and when you finish reading the first scroll with God's words, tie a stone to it and throw it into the midst of the Euphrates, and say, 'Thus shall Babylon sink, to rise no more, because of the disaster that I am bringing upon her, and they shall become exhausted.' "[66]

"Have you written down those last words anywhere?" asked Seraiah.

"No," I replied. "There aren't very many and if you can't learn them now, you will have to write them down yourself. I'm sure Baruch will have some papyrus you could write on, and you can add the rest of the instructions too, if you want to."

"I think I will," he said. "Baruch, do you have a sheet of papyrus?"

"Yes," said Baruch, "and you might as well come and sit at my workbench; the ink and pens are there, too."

We walked together into the small room in which Baruch worked as a scribe, and he pulled back the stool from underneath the workbench for Seraiah to sit on. Taking a clean sheet of papyrus from the bench, he handed it to Seraiah, then he took a pen and an inkwell and put them in front of him.

"So, first I read the scroll. Is that right?" Seraiah looked at me inquiringly.

"Yes," I confirmed. "The bigger scroll, the one with God's messages."

---

[65] Jeremiah 51:62
[66] Jeremiah 51:59-64

Seraiah made a note on his papyrus and then continued, "After that, I say the words from the second scroll. I have to learn those ones, don't I?"

"That's right. And you can do what you want with that scroll once you have finished."

Seraiah made more notes. "Next comes the stone, doesn't it?"

"Yes, tie a stone to that big scroll and throw it into the middle of the river Euphrates."

More notes and then Seraiah asked, "Then you need to tell me the final words to speak as the scroll sinks. What are they?"

"The words are, 'Thus shall Babylon sink, to rise no more, because of the disaster that I am bringing upon her, and they shall become exhausted.' "[67]

"Thus… shall… Babylon… sink…," Seraiah repeated slowly as he wrote the words carefully on the papyrus. When he had finished the sentence, he said, "I really like that last part, anyway. And the parts of God's words that I skimmed through sound good too."

"They do indeed," I agreed, and Baruch was nodding with us. "So just make sure that you are very careful to do exactly what I have told you. God doesn't give instructions for nothing. Make sure you get them right."

"I'll do my level best," said Seraiah.

☙

July, 594 BC – the 4th year of King Zedekiah

It happened!

The rumours going around the city had suggested that it was going to happen, but I just couldn't believe that

---

[67] Jeremiah 51:59-64

King Zedekiah would ever do such a dishonest and downright foolish thing as to break his word to Nebuchadnezzar and rebel.

The false prophets had been whispering lies in his ear ever since the Chaldean "advisors" left. Unfortunately, though they had confidence, it was a completely misplaced conceit.

Maybe I had even unwittingly contributed to the problem.

Seraiah had carefully taken the scroll I had given him all the way to Babylon. On his arrival, he had read it aloud and duly thrown it into the river. The entire process had gone well, and there had been no adverse reaction from anyone, although Seraiah reported that there had been many people listening as he read God's words, finishing as they did by predicting utter destruction for Babylon and highlighting the pointlessness of human empires:

"Thus says the Lord of hosts:
The broad wall of Babylon
shall be levelled to the ground,
and her high gates shall be burned with fire.
The peoples labour for nothing,
and the nations weary themselves only for fire."[68]

However, it seemed that the message had been too convincing, too encouraging to the people who were fomenting rebellion. They heard the words and saw hope. Babylon was to be destroyed! God's timing of 70 years was forgotten and some other words God had spoken were taken and twisted to suggest a much shorter time. Within months, I would be having to cope with the results of this over-exuberance of rebellion.

---

[68] Jeremiah 51:58

For the moment, however, things were bad enough. By the time Zedekiah arrived back in Jerusalem, he was almost decided. The humiliation of bowing down before Nebuchadnezzar while all of the court looked on had smarted badly. Nebuchadnezzar's interrogation regarding Zedekiah's delay in making the journey to Babylon, his questions as to the economic progress of little Judah, and the stunning opulence of his throne room had combined to make a frustrated Zedekiah long to pick up one of the wine-filled golden goblets that was offered to him and throw it into the face of his tormentor. With significant time to think on the long journey back to Judah, Zedekiah's fury at these perceived insults had grown, and his advisors had done nothing to calm him down or keep his folly in check: instead, they had encouraged it.

Only a few days after the return of the royal party, Zedekiah had announced that Judah was once more an independent kingdom. Judah, he declared, would choose its own way.

Zedekiah had broken his promise to Nebuchadnezzar the king of Babylon – the promise he had confirmed with an oath taken in the name of Yahweh, the God of Israel.

No more reports would be sent – despite his promises. No more deferential visits would be made to the great conqueror – despite his earlier acknowledgement of Nebuchadnezzar as his overlord.

This was how God assessed Zedekiah's rebellion.

But the picture Zedekiah's advisors had painted for their king, the picture which finally convinced their lord how he should act, was quite different – and they painted it with precision and conviction.

No more demeaning reports should be sent as from a servant to his master, explaining his every action; no more debasing visits made to an arrogant conqueror in his elaborate halls; no more gold sent to line Nebuchad-nezzar's throne room and fill his treasuries.

The fourth year of King Zedekiah, they said, would go down in history as the time when Judah finally asserted her independence and claimed the promises of God. A king sitting on the throne of David would rule in God's promised land.

The entire picture was utter nonsense.

What God saw was a man who could not be trusted to keep his word. A man who would rebel against God and break the solemn oath he had sworn. Zedekiah was a liar.

In that fourth year of Zedekiah, God told me to revisit a parable that I had presented to King Jehoiakim a few years into his reign. Returning to our house in Anathoth, I found the wooden yoke that I had made – fortunately, it had not been damaged by the Chaldeans during the latest invasion. It took only a short time clean it up and to repair the slight damage that ten years had wrought on the straps. Soon the yoke was ready to wear again. I wondered if anyone would remember it.

Despite my invitation to my mother for her to live in my house in Jerusalem, she had moved back to Anathoth and was enjoying the quietness there – compared with the noise and bustle of Jerusalem. While I was cleaning up my yoke, I told her that I believed she should come and stay with me in Jerusalem. I explained what King Zedekiah had done and that we could expect a savage response from Babylon sometime. I did not believe that Jerusalem would be a safe place, but felt that Anathoth would be even more dangerous. How I longed for an instruction from God to leave Jerusalem, leave Judah, run away and find a place of safety. But God had been faithful to me throughout my life – how could I now be unfaithful to him? My mother said that she would think about it, and I urged her to act quickly, feeling that Nebuchadnezzar's response would be swift. Yet again, I was wrong.

God had commanded me to present the parable to Zedekiah and all the city, so I wore my yoke all the way back from Anathoth. As I entered the gate of Jerusalem, the guards looked at me blankly. Of course, every one of these guards had been appointed by Zedekiah, as the former guards had all been taken captive to Babylon. I walked through the streets towards my house and many eyes looked at me in wonder, but in none did I see any flicker of recognition or memory. Once again, it reminded me of just how much the city had changed. Nebuchadnezzar's two deportations had taken away so much of the city. Most of the people I had known before had gone, and this parable would be new to all of the newcomers. Would even the king recognise it?

I made an appointment with King Zedekiah, though it took quite a few days to get past the wall his advisors tried to build to keep me out. However, God's promise held, and when I persisted and stood firm against them, I was finally allowed to see the king. I had refused to give any indication of what I wanted to say, and many of Zedekiah's so-called friends were present when I was led into the throne room and told the king that I had a message from Yahweh for him.

"Speak," he prompted me, so I spoke the words of God:

> "Bring your necks under the yoke
> of the king of Babylon,
> and serve him and his people and live.
> Why will you and your people die
> by the sword, by famine, and by pestilence,
> as the Lord has spoken concerning any nation
> that will not serve the king of Babylon?
> Do not listen to the words of the prophets

who are saying to you,
'You shall not serve the king of Babylon,'
for it is a lie that they are prophesying to you.
I have not sent them, declares the Lord,
but they are prophesying falsely in my name,
with the result that I will drive you out
and you will perish,
you and the prophets who are prophesying to you."[69]

From the very start, there was a low rumble of voices and dissent in the background. By the end, it was becoming difficult to make myself heard, but I finished anyway. The king's advisors and the so-called prophets who stood around the room looked surprised and angry. Zedekiah himself looked unsure. I faced them all with an immovable stare, and, yet again, God took care of me. Without God's protection, I am sure that I would not have escaped that throne room alive. I was to have an increasing need of God's protection over the next few years.

I left the throne room with no hope that Zedekiah would change his path. There would be no sudden sending of mounted messengers to withdraw the earlier messages of rebellion. The decision was irreversible because there was no-one strong enough to admit that God's way was right.

Once outside the palace, I spoke to the priests and to all the people in the temple courts and at various gates of the city, saying,

"Thus says the Lord:
Do not listen to the words of your prophets
who are prophesying to you, saying,
'Behold, the vessels of the Lord's house
will now shortly be brought back from Babylon,'
for it is a lie that they are prophesying to you.

---

[69] Jeremiah 27:12-15

Do not listen to them; serve the king of Babylon and live.
Why should this city become a desolation?"[70]

Sullen crowds heard my words, but did not listen to them.   No-one could see any future in telling Nebuchadnezzar that we would again submit.   The prophets were all saying that Nebuchadnezzar would lose his power and that no retribution would come as a result of this rebellion.

My final warning was about the items in the temple:
"Thus says the Lord of hosts,
the God of Israel,
concerning the vessels that are left
in the house of the Lord,
in the house of the king of Judah, and in Jerusalem:
They shall be carried to Babylon and remain there
until the day when I visit them, declares the Lord.
Then I will bring them back
and restore them to this place."[71]

Would the people listen? I didn't know for certain, but I doubted it. What I hadn't even considered was that they might take God's words and twist them to suit their own ends.

---

[70] Jeremiah 27:16-17
[71] Jeremiah 27:21-22

Chapter 12

Hananiah

August, 594 BC – the 4th year of King Zedekiah

God's instruction to Zedekiah was ignored. I suspect that he did not have the courage to reverse his decision in the face of his friends' and advisors' opinions. Sadly, Zedekiah was never willing to lead, or to take a firm public stand on anything that had not been approved by others. The contrast with his father Josiah could not have been more marked.

I continued to wear my wooden yoke as God had instructed me, a silent reminder to all that God intended our nation to be subject to Babylon. I was amazed how much anger it seemed to generate. More and more people seemed to sneer at me as I walked past. The advocates of rebellion had won the battle for the hearts of the people, and it was clear that the priests in the temple were also on the side of the rebels. I didn't exactly feel unsafe, but I never felt very welcome either.

Meanwhile, false prophets spoke with more and more confidence. They even began to weave the words of God into their hopeful predictions.

One particular man who did this was Hananiah the son of Azzur. He was from Gibeon and had come to Jerusalem some time after King Jeconiah had been taken away. He called himself a prophet.

Now God had spoken to me about Babylon, saying:

"Go out of the midst of her, my people!
Let every one save his life
from the fierce anger of the Lord!
Let not your heart faint, and be not fearful
at the report heard in the land,
when a report comes in one year
and afterward a report in another year,
and violence is in the land,
and ruler is against ruler."[72]

The words were quite obscure, but seemed to relate to the time when the captives were to leave Babylon and return to Israel. Exactly what they meant, I was not sure, but I was sure that they did not mean what Hananiah took from them. He latched on to the line that said "when a report comes in one year and afterward a report in another year" and began to claim that the captivity would be over in only two years!

Then one day during the fifth month, he sent me a message asking me to come and meet him in the temple courts on the following day, in what turned out to be a set-up – although it took me a while to realise it. I arrived in the temple the next day at the appointed time, but instead of finding Hananiah alone, I found quite a crowd waiting in the court where he had asked me to meet him: a group of priests and many others. I felt a little unsure,

---

[72] Jeremiah 51:45-46

concerned that I might be interrupting some organised gathering that I hadn't heard about, so I walked hesitantly up to Hananiah, still wearing my yoke. He was standing on the steps that led up to the temple, talking to a few others, with the crowd spread out in front of him.

"Hananiah," I said uncertainly, "this was the time at which you wanted to meet me, wasn't it? I hope I'm not interrupting something else?"

"Oh no, Jeremiah," he replied, smiling knowingly, "you're not interrupting anything. In fact, now that you are here, we can begin."

He turned to the crowd and called for quiet. Unsure what to do, I waited to see what would happen.

Well, it was all a performance. Hananiah wanted an audience for his prophecies, and for some reason he wanted me there too. I felt rather lost for a while, and stood there silently as he announced to the crowd that he had received special messages from Yahweh, the God of Israel, who had told him to deliver them in the temple and to make sure that I was present to hear them too. Although he didn't say it in so many words, he clearly implied that God wanted me to hear his message and to admit that the messages I had been delivering were not really from him.

Looking back on it, I think Hananiah wanted me there for two main purposes: firstly to lend him some credibility, since almost everyone in Jerusalem knew me as a prophet; and secondly to ridicule me, as I stood there in my yoke looking bewildered, while he confidently presented a message that would be popular with the people and had the support of many of the leading priests. Looking around, I was pleased to see at least that neither Azariah nor Gemariah was in the crowd, although some of my other close relatives were present.

Hananiah

Once Hananiah had got the crowd's attention, he quieted them and began to speak, explaining that he had a message from God to pass on to them. His voice was deep and powerful, pleasant to the ear, and very convincing. Some in the crowd had obviously heard from him before, because they settled themselves down on the pavement with looks of anticipation on their faces. The fifth month is the middle of our summer, and the mid-morning sun that day was hot as always. Some of the audience found a little shade in the shadows of the walls and columns, but most just covered their heads to give them a little protection from the sun.

When everyone seemed ready, Hananiah smiled around at the crowd, looking slowly from man to man as he gradually lifted his arms up towards heaven, then began, "Thus says the Lord of hosts, the God of Israel: I have broken the yoke of the king of Babylon." He formed his hands into fists and brought them down savagely. "Within two years," he continued, speaking the words slowly, and holding up two fingers of his right hand so that all of the crowd could see them, "I will bring back to this place all the vessels of the Lord's house, which Nebuchadnezzar king of Babylon took away from this place and carried to Babylon." Cheering broke out from the crowd, and Hananiah acknowledged their approval, but waited for the crowd to calm down before continuing, "I will also bring back to this place Jeconiah the son of Jehoiakim, king of Judah, and all the exiles from Judah who went to Babylon, declares the Lord, for I will break the yoke of the king of Babylon."[73]

It was a performance alright, and he finished with his arms bent up in front of his chest, his hands balled into fists as if he had personally broken a yoke from off the neck of an ox.

---

[73] Jeremiah 28:2-4

I wasn't sure what to do. His message was quite different from what God had said to me. Why would God change his message unless there was some repentance? – and I had seen no signs of repentance in Jerusalem. Nevertheless, I was only a prophet, a mouthpiece; any message of denial or condemnation must come from God. In the meantime, until any message might come, all I could do was to encourage people to reflect on how God had spoken to his people over the centuries. "Amen!" I said. "May the Lord do so; may the Lord make the words that you have prophesied come true, and bring back to this place from Babylon the vessels of the house of the Lord, and all the exiles. Yet hear now this word that I speak in your hearing and in the hearing of all the people. The prophets who preceded you and me from ancient times prophesied war, famine, and pestilence against many countries and great kingdoms. As for the prophet who prophesies peace, when the word of that prophet comes to pass, then it will be known that the Lord has truly sent the prophet."[74]

Hananiah was far from pleased to hear any suggestion that there could be doubt about his prophecy. He stepped towards me and for a moment I thought he was attacking me, but he only reached for my yoke bars. I tried to stop him, but he was a tall, strong man and had the advantage of surprise. He brushed aside my resisting hands, untied the yoke from my neck and removed it.

Holding it up above his head, he grasped the yoke bars firmly and tore them apart, breaking the yoke in pieces.[75] Theatrically, he flung the pieces down and announced, "Thus says the Lord: Even so will I break the

---

[74] Jeremiah 28:5-9
[75] Jeremiah 28:10

yoke of Nebuchadnezzar king of Babylon from the neck of all the nations within two years."[76]

There was nothing more that I could do or say. I left.

I don't know whether Hananiah genuinely believed the words he spoke or not. Was his aim merely to gain acknowledgement and admiration? History speaks for itself: what he prophesied did not happen – but did he believe that it would?

❧

A few days after the encounter with Hananiah, I heard several pieces of news that were important to me.

King Jeconiah had apparently been established in a special prison in Babylon, along with his family. That was interesting in itself, because it was an unexpectedly generous way of treating a captured king. Was it because he had surrendered to Nebuchadnezzar instead of continuing to resist?

God's operation is often so subtle that it is hard to be sure how minutely he controls events in the lives of individuals and nations.

However, that was not the only news about Jeconiah that seemed related to the fulfilment of prophecy. Apparently, Jeconiah's closest supervisors were a group of soldiers from Judah! They had agreed to work for Nebuchadnezzar and to supervise the royal family in their prison, enforcing Nebuchadnezzar's rules. And these soldiers were the very ones whose company Jeconiah as king had often sought out – probably largely as a small sign of rebellion against his overbearing mother, whose ideas of a clear class separation would always have kept her from even speaking to such men. Jeconiah had made

---

[76] Jeremiah 28:11

friends of them, and now they were his supervisors. From the reports I heard, he was very hurt and angry that his "friends" should have betrayed him in such a way.

It seemed to me to provide a clear answer to the question God had asked:

"What will you say when they set as head over you
those whom you yourself have taught
to be friends to you?
Will not pangs take hold of you
like those of a woman in labour?"[77]

So much for Jeconiah's "low-born friends", as his mother viewed them! However, the statement seemed to have been directed at both Jeconiah and his mother, so I wondered how it was being fulfilled for her. Unfortunately, we prophets often don't get to see the fulfilment of the words God speaks through us. I never heard how Nehushta had to endure the fulfilment of that prophecy.

Another piece of news was heartbreaking to me. It had gradually become apparent that the cost of Nebuchadnezzar's invasion had been even higher than anyone had realised. Innocent people had been killed all over Judah and Israel, particularly in the south. Then as the Chaldean army had travelled north, many people had been killed incidentally, not for any particular reason, but simply because the Chaldeans were cruel; not as the sad outcome of some grand battle or courageous resistance, but killed in cold blood.

I learned that two of those who had been tragically killed in this way were Shobai and Maacah. I had loved them dearly, although I had never been able to spend as much time with them as I would have liked. It happened like this. Miriam, Maacah's mother, had died some years

---

[77] Jeremiah 13:21

before at a good old age, having gradually wheezed and struggled more and more as the years passed. A reliable helper had taken care of most of the work at her inn in Bethel for many years, while Miriam had gradually done less and less. Indeed, for the last ten years or so, she had never climbed the stairs of the inn, but had limited herself to life on the ground floor. With her death, Shobai and Maacah had taken over the inn, particularly the cooking, but had kept on the faithful helper for most of the other work.

When the Chaldean soldiers came, some of them were looking for trouble. Maacah had been cooking in the kitchen while Shobai kept the peace in the main room where the guests ate. I was sure that his ever-present smile and welcoming presence would have helped him greatly, but even so, there came a moment where he could no longer control the violence that endeared itself to the Chaldean soldiers. The faithful helper – I never even learned her name – did something to upset one of the soldiers. She was a stern, serious woman, and it may have been something as simple as a look of disapproval at a soldier's fluent cursing. Whatever the cause, the soldier felt insulted and was eager to make someone pay. Shobai's attempts to make peace apparently made him the target, and the shouting brought Maacah from the kitchen. Within moments, the shouting had changed to violence and both Shobai and Maacah were dead, while the stern, serious woman who had been the spark that had lit the fire of death was left in shock to serve a meal to the murderers. The next day, the soldiers had moved on.

Three weeks had passed and nothing had happened about Hananiah. I can tell you, it made me wonder. Shobai and Maacah – a couple who loved Yahweh – were dead, yet Hananiah was overbearingly alive.

His confidence had grown with the enthusiastic welcome his prophecies had received and my lame response. He became bolder, until it was common to hear him in the temple propounding his version of the future.

One day, as I sat reading a scroll of very dubious prophecy in the fading light of a long summer evening, I was feeling quite angry about people who make up prophecies and foist them on a gullible nation. The scroll had been brought from Israel many years before and claimed that God would deliver Samaria from the besieging Assyrians. It must have been written during the siege that led to the final destruction of Samaria and the carrying away into exile of the ten tribes of Israel. Really, it was very similar to the prophecies of Hananiah, with the same desperate, but hopeless, predictions of salvation. Somehow, this scroll had survived that siege, but as part of my ongoing task of reviewing our so-called religious scrolls, I was destroying it. Although it claimed to be the words of Yahweh, it was clearly a fraud. Quite apart from the fact that it had proved to be wrong, it also contained the giveaway teaching of tolerance of immorality and idol worship.

I was angry and wanted God's judgement to fall on evil people like Hananiah and the ancient writer of this scroll from Israel. I cut the scroll in pieces, lit a lamp and held the first piece in the small flame. Slowly, the flame licked over the section I held and began to creep along the edge in threads of fire. Suddenly, as the flame spread, I felt the fire of God spreading within me as well.[78] The fire inside spread much more quickly and felt much hotter than my little flame that was consuming the false prophecies I had just read. Then the voice of God spoke

---

[78] We do not know exactly when God gave this message to Jeremiah. Hananiah's original message was given in the fifth month, and this was "sometime after" (Jeremiah 28:12).

within the fire:

> "Go, tell Hananiah, 'Thus says the Lord:
> You have broken wooden bars,
> but you have made in their place bars of iron.
> For thus says the Lord of hosts, the God of Israel:
> I have put upon the neck of all these nations
> an iron yoke to serve
> Nebuchadnezzar king of Babylon,
> and they shall serve him,
> for I have given to him
> even the beasts of the field.' "[79]

God's voice continued as he pronounced his judgement on Hananiah, and I was thankful that the man's presumption would not be left unanswered. If no answer had been given, nothing would have discouraged the people from following such foolish dreams. I slept a happier sleep that night than I had since Hananiah had spoken.

It wasn't hard to find Hananiah the next day as he spoke to his band of followers in the temple, but it was less easy to keep him quiet while I spoke. Eventually, though, he let me speak without competition, and I relayed the words of God, including the punishment God had assigned him:

"Listen, Hananiah, the Lord has not sent you, and you have made this people trust in a lie. Therefore thus says the Lord:

> 'Behold, I will remove you
> from the face of the earth.
> This year you shall die,
> because you have uttered rebellion
> against the Lord.' "[80]

---

[79] Jeremiah 28:13-14
[80] Jeremiah 28:15-16

⧉

October, 594 BC – the 4th year of King Zedekiah

It didn't take long for God's judgement to be carried out. Within a month, in the seventh month of the year, as autumn began to cool the days and lengthen the nights, the prophet Hananiah died.

⧉

Hananiah's death dropped me down yet another rung in my family's esteem. Like our father, Azariah trumpeted tolerance as one of God's great attributes, and the death of a false prophet did not please him.

Quite simply, Azariah blamed me for Hananiah's death.

Arguing that it was exactly what God had warned in the Book of the Law[81] that he would do to false prophets did not convince him.

Even Gemariah blamed me, and would no longer speak to me peaceably.

My relatives from Anathoth joined in the criticism of me, and I felt completely alone.

Hananiah's relatives also blamed me, and there was no question that their feelings towards me were pure hatred. That was to cause me a lot of trouble later. In fact, it almost cost me my life.

In the recent past, I had lost my friends Shobai and Maacah, attracted hatred from a false prophet and his family, and united my own family against me.

Only my mother gave me any support. However, my mother was old and the summer had been hard for her.

---

[81] Deuteronomy 18:20

She was beginning to show her advanced age. Just before the death of the false prophet Hananiah, her health had finally forced her to agree to come and live with me.

Without her support, I don't know what I would have done. But even her support could not be very vocal, for she was an old woman and had a deep longing for her family to live in peace, not to be torn apart by hatred.

Little did I know that, despite my mother's gentle support, the situation was soon to get even worse.

Chapter 13

Once again, we waited...

Zedekiah's shameless rebellion did not prompt any immediate response from powerful Babylon. Instead, Nebuchadnezzar continued his work of empire building on other, more important fronts. Brutal repression crushed all resistance along many of the frontiers of his ever-widening kingdom.

Once again, little Judah remained unfinished business, left for a time, but not forgotten – yet despite the respite, no change for the better occurred in Judah over the next few years.

Zedekiah's uninspiring reign continued. When I spoke with him alone, as I had done on a few occasions during his reign, he seemed quite a pleasant character. Unfortunately, however, he seemed to have a habit of choosing bad friends and listening to their evil opinions far too much. As I mentioned earlier, it was obvious to everyone that he was much happier following than leading; parroting the opinions of others instead of having his own opinions and sticking to them. He was not completely happy with the behaviour and opinions of his friends, but he would not direct them in better ways.

Such a character should never be a king: he will not reign for himself, and the sorts of men and women he attracts as advisors will bring disaster to a kingdom.

This was the path Zedekiah was following.

Idol worship spread even further through the city and seemed likely to completely take over the temple too. Early in Zedekiah's fifth year I reached the age of 51 and therefore was no longer eligible to work as a priest in the temple. No doubt my brother and his associates heaved a sigh of relief that I could no longer claim the right to work as an active priest and complain incessantly about the corruption, ignorance and evil that pervaded every corner of the priesthood. But I wasn't sorry either – the task had taken its toll on me and I was glad to step back a little. Although I had spent quite a lot of time away from Jerusalem on God's errands, and had been excluded from the temple at times in a bid to shut me up, nevertheless the twenty years in which I had been eligible to work as a priest had been hard work, and I was exhausted.

By the fifth year of Zedekiah's reign, the typical divisions in society that had been broken down by Nebuchadnezzar's removal of the leaders, the rich, and the skilled workers, were well established again. The new rich had the king's ear and grew ever richer. The poor grew ever poorer, and most ended up under obligation to some rich man just to get enough to survive.

Nebuchadnezzar and his army had left many widows, fatherless children and orphans in the city, but now most of them were virtually slaves.

Disaster was coming – I knew that – but for those few years it didn't seem to be in any hurry to arrive. Nebuchadnezzar had not returned and utter destruction was not obviously hanging over our heads. The neighbouring nations were making threats and sending frequent raiding parties that attacked and troubled the land, but the nation seemed to consider that a small problem compared with the trouble the Chaldean army had brought. Not only that, but the cost of those raiding parties was paid much more by those in country areas, and that did not concern the king and his nobles as much as it should have done.

In such comparative peace, the rich and arrogant grew increasingly confident that God's threats were empty and meaningless.

Despite the death of Hananiah, the people still preferred to believe his prophecies. Even as the two-year time limit he had placed on his own prophecies drew near without any signs of a return of either people or goods from Babylon, God's words were still ignored.

I had been confident that the people must listen eventually. Surely in this time of advanced knowledge, people must be reasonable and logical enough to see that if a man died as God had said he would and his prophecies never came to pass, then it made sense to pay attention to God's words rather than those of self-seeking liars.

But I was wrong.

Reason and logic had no part in those people's thinking.

Once again, if anyone thought about God's prophecy regarding the death of Hananiah at all, it was only to argue that God had said he would die "within a year". Hananiah, they argued, had died within a month – far too quickly for it to have been God's work! Now I ask you, how can people call that logic?

Blind, deaf, stubborn, stupid, illogical, irrational, inexplicable, unnatural, wilful, obstinate, perverse; the descriptions of my people that filled my head each day were never complimentary, and all of them reflected the deep sense of anger and frustration that filled me. As I watched and fretted, I was often angry enough to want to kill many of the unthinking fools who said that Yahweh would never punish.

I find it utterly impossible to describe just how great my anger was whenever I thought about my people's response to Yahweh's entreaties, his warnings, his threats and finally his promises of destruction. At times, I wished that I had received the sort of prophet's commission that God had described for Elisha; it had finished with:

> "…and the one who escapes from the sword of Jehu
> shall Elisha put to death."[82]

However, that was not God's plan for me. Instead, mine was the part of a constant, carping critic, never backing down but endlessly repeating God's warnings to an unheeding nation. God had appointed me a tester of metals for my people, one who would assess their value, not one who would punish.[83] That was God's work, and he was much more patient with my people than I would have been.

When the time for punishment finally came, and Jerusalem burned like a torch, I saw enough and more than enough of the punishment that had waited so long to come.

But in the meantime, I fretted and longed for God's action.

CR

If the overall behaviour in the city was going downhill, the religious behaviour was no better. Sexual immorality was

---

[82] 1 Kings 19:17
[83] Jeremiah 6:27-30

becoming more and more common, and so was the unfaithfulness in worship that God has so often likened to unfaithfulness in marriage.

You would expect there to be an outcry about this from the priests and Levites in the temple, but my brother and the entire hierarchy remained stubbornly silent on the subject. In fact, some even seemed to enthusiastically join in.

By the sixth year of Zedekiah I was sure that Azariah's dislike of me had matured into full-fledged hatred, yet even I was treated with some of the tolerance that he so vocally supported.

Worshippers of the sun were tolerated and even welcomed by him; likewise, I was tolerated even though I repeatedly reiterated God's comments about obedience to his laws and the keeping of the Sabbath.

ℭ

September, 592 BC – the 6th year of King Zedekiah

One Sabbath, the trade of the city being in full swing as it always was, I stood at the Benjamin Gate, finishing God's announcement of the stark choice the nation was making every week about the Sabbath:

" '…if you do not listen to me,
to keep the Sabbath day holy,
and not to bear a burden
and enter by the gates of Jerusalem on the Sabbath day,
then I will kindle a fire in its gates,
and it shall devour the palaces of Jerusalem
and shall not be quenched.' "[84]

As the last words of God's frightening warning

---

[84] Jeremiah 17:27

echoed across the open market area, filled as it was with buyers and sellers, I saw my brother approaching. He was accompanied by a group of other senior priests and his dress proclaimed his exalted position as God's High Priest.

A lesser priest whom I did not recognise, probably some 15 years my junior, was walking in front of the group and arrived first. He looked at me contemptuously and immediately began his attack: "Jeremiah, the High Priest has received complaints about you from princes, prophets, priests and the people. Your words are divisive, setting people of different faiths against each other. You claim that you are the only one who knows truth. That attitude is bigoted and destructive. When will you cease your self-promotion?"

"Has the High Priest received complaints from God about my behaviour?" I countered, firmly, but not aggressively. "If he has, that would be important. But complaints from those about whom God himself complains are not to be listened to. Of course, God's High Priest will know that very well." I glanced across at Azariah, who had arrived by then, complete with his entourage. A crowd was gathering around us, as had obviously been planned. Azariah's eyes showed irritation, but also a calm confidence that the scene would play out as they had arranged. We were surrounded by about fifty or a hundred people by that time, and Azariah looked around before speaking to make sure that everyone was ready to hear his words.

"Jeremiah," he began, looking at me almost as if he didn't know me, "here in Jerusalem we maintain the temple of Yahweh, the house that he has consecrated and in which he said he has put his name forever."[85] His voice was smooth and confident, filled with warmth and encouragement, and reminded me strongly of our father.

---

[85] 1 Kings 9:3

He had referred to God's words to Solomon, but I was certain he would not mention the conditions that God placed on that promise. God had added a big "if", and had gone on to promise that should Solomon or his children stop obeying God's commands or worship other gods instead, then he would destroy the house and leave it in ruins.[86]

I was right. Azariah continued, "Since the temple is the house of God and since Jerusalem is the city of peace, it is incumbent upon us to keep God's peace, to welcome all who would come to his temple and not to insist on our own narrow interpretation of his words. You have had your time as a priest of Yahweh. You have worked hard. We have not always seen eye to eye in what you have done, but you have done what you believed you should. Now it is for others to continue the work and to build on the peace that God has graciously given us."

"Peace?" I asked incredulously, "Do you call it 'peace' when the nations around attack our countryside incessantly, when the king's friends and those in power fill this city with blood, and when violence and immorality are so common that men cannot leave their wives at night without fearing for their safety? Is it peace when the certainty of Nebuchadnezzar's return hangs over our heads like one of his own catapult stones, coming closer every day? You say 'Peace, peace', but there is no peace!"[87]

☙

That day I was rather despondent as I returned home.

My mother had been unwell for a week or so, and although she seemed to be getting better, I did not want

---

[86] 1 Kings 9:4-9
[87] Jeremiah 6:14; 8:11

to burden her with my problems. I was concerned about her health and wondered whether she would recover at all at her age, or was coming to the end of her life. I prepared the food we were to eat and then sat with her in her room as we ate. I was pleased to see that she showed more interest in her food than she had done the previous night.

We talked for a while, and then she asked me what was wrong. I had thought that I was hiding my feelings well, but my mother had always been able to read me as if my thoughts were written on my face. I told her that it was nothing important, and changed the subject. The look on her face showed that she didn't believe me, but she was still tired from her sickness and let the matter drop.

After a while, I said good night to her, and she advised me to go to bed and sleep on it, adding that if the problem still looked like a problem in the morning, then maybe we could talk about it.

Instead, I went into my room and sat and thought. Nothing seemed to be very fair. All of the better men I had known had been either killed or taken into captivity. Jerusalem was filled with evil, and the evil people seemed to be becoming more and more powerful while the weak were trodden underfoot. I was being picked on by friends, family and enemies alike. As I thought, I gradually fell into prayer:

> "Righteous are you, O Lord,
> when I complain to you;
> yet I would plead my case before you.
> Why does the way of the wicked prosper?
> Why do all who are treacherous thrive?
> You plant them, and they take root;
> they grow and produce fruit;
> you are near in their mouth
> and far from their heart.
> But you, O Lord, know me; you see me,
> and test my heart toward you.

Pull them out like sheep for the slaughter,
and set them apart for the day of slaughter.
How long will the land mourn
and the grass of every field wither?
For the evil of those who dwell in it
the beasts and the birds are swept away,
because they said,
'He will not see our latter end.' "[88]

For a time, it felt better to have got the complaints off my chest. I realise that God knows my thoughts before I even have them and that he understands the mixed-up flow of thoughts, but I prefer my prayers to be presented in a more ordered way if I can. On this occasion, it was a subject I have thought about often, but rarely commit to specific prayer because it feels unreasonable to complain against the God who understands everything while I struggle even to understand why I can feel happy one day and sad the next without anything seeming to have happened to cause the change.

Having committed my problems to God, I began to ready myself for sleep. But then, as I blew out the lamp and lay down, I felt a gentle breeze stir in the room and a quiet voice spoke, whether in my mind or in the room, I don't know. The voice was clear as crystal, and every word felt almost as if it had a special value and life of its own:

"If you have raced with men on foot,
and they have wearied you,
how will you compete with horses?
And if in a safe land you are so trusting,
what will you do in the thicket of the Jordan?
For even your brothers and the house of your father,
even they have dealt treacherously with you;
they are in full cry after you;

---

[88] Jeremiah 12:1-4

do not believe them,
though they speak friendly words to you.

"I have forsaken my house;
I have abandoned my heritage;
I have given the beloved of my soul
into the hands of her enemies.
My heritage has become to me
like a lion in the forest;
she has lifted up her voice against me;
therefore I hate her."[89]

It was a long time before I fell asleep that night, as I puzzled over the words and wondered why God's presence had felt so different from normal. God's words had continued for only a short time, so it was no long and convoluted message, nevertheless, I could not grasp the meaning without protracted and determined thought.

Eventually I sank into a fitful sleep, no longer any more content than I had been before voicing my complaints to God. Instead, I recalled the vision God had shown me when my friends had plotted to kill me. This warning about my family sounded frighteningly similar – had my brothers and my relatives really been behaving treacherously against me without me realising it? Did they want to kill me too? Had they made plans to do so? Had the concerted approach that day been intended to culminate in my death? Or was that stage of the plan still to come? If I tried to sum up God's words in speaking of my family, they seemed to say, "Grow up! What did you expect but that your family would want to kill you?" God also seemed to link it to his own response in abandoning his temple. He was hated, so I could expect to be hated myself. His children had rejected him, so why should I be surprised that my family would try to kill me?

---

[89] Jeremiah 12:5-8

It was a chilling thought and I wondered how many of God's prophets had had to learn this terrifying lesson.

❧

After this response from God – which felt very much like a rebuke – I felt even more isolated than before.

I paid close attention to my interactions with my brothers and my relatives, and it became clear to me that God (of course) was absolutely right. If they could have found a way to kill me, they would have done so. As it was, they tried. Without God to protect me, I would never have lived to see the ongoing degradation of the temple which had once been God's house but which he had now abandoned.

The empty shell remained, but how long would it last?

The sixth year of Zedekiah had shown that Hananiah's prophecies were false, but it was not until the eighth year of Zedekiah that God's assurances that Nebuchadnezzar would return began to show their irresistible truth.

Suddenly it came, and Jerusalem was abuzz with the news: Nebuchadnezzar was coming back.

Chapter 14

Another siege

April, 589 BC – the 9th year of King Zedekiah

Parties of scouts kept King Zedekiah informed as the Chaldean army moved south, first into Israel and then into Judah.   There was no surprise this time as Nebuchadnezzar's army approached Jerusalem.

No surprise perhaps, but it was still a time of terror. Nebuchadnezzar's army moved rapidly through Israel, burning and killing. Many abandoned their homes and fled before them. Smoke on the horizon announced their coming and fleeing peasants added substance to the reports. All who came spoke of brutality and profligate violence, of men and women burning on pyres that were the ruins of their homes, of crowds on roads overtaken by men on horseback who had ridden over men, women and children alike, slashing and hacking until none were left alive save a lucky few who had found a temporary refuge behind rocks or in caves or holes in the earth. Some told of torture, and others of rape.

Some fled to towns, seeking safety within stone walls, but such was the terror that preceded the Chaldean army that when they approached a town, the inhabitants would open the gates and flee.[90]

In many towns, only the aged, the weak, the sick, the expectant mothers ready to give birth and the very young remained, and the soldiers wasted little time on them: clubs, swords and spears disposed of all, young or old, without mercy. Unborn babies died with the rest as their terror-stricken mothers were ripped open with unmitigated cruelty.

Inexorably the soldiers moved on, bringing death wherever they went. Cities and towns were swiftly taken and any unwise resistance brought the punishment of still greater devastation.

Blood flowed almost without limit, and the roads were flooded with hysterical refugees.

People fled to well-known caves, only to find that their welcoming darkness was already filled with other frantic citizens, desperate to make sure that no Chaldean soldiers were led to their hiding place. Late arrivals were forced to leave their hoped-for place of safety once more and flee further south.

Many of those who lived in quiet country cottages amid wide acres of farming land heard rumours and whispers of the coming terror, but brushed them off in the face of urgent farm deadlines. Often, for them, death came suddenly as rampaging soldiers gathered entire families together and forced them into their own cottages, to which the soldiers then set fire. Any who sought to flee the flames were met with unrelenting savagery.

---

[90] Jeremiah 4:29

In Judah, the small window of opportunity had been put to productive use. Frantic activity in both the countryside and the city had made certain that Jerusalem was well stocked with food and water in preparation for a prolonged siege. Weapons and ammunition had been stockpiled as well: huge quantities of slingstones had been brought into the city and lay in large piles against the walls, easily accessible for the defenders on the walls.

Large quantities of additional stone had also been brought in to provide extra support for the city gates. Heavy battering rams could quickly destroy even the strongest wooden gates, and the only way to avoid catastrophic damage was to fill up the empty spaces behind the gates with piles of stones.

The finishing touches were being placed on plans for the defence of the city as Nebuchadnezzar's army moved relentlessly through Israel. At the same time, crowds of people hurried down the roads to Jerusalem and sought refuge within her massive walls. Surely those walls were impenetrable? And did not everyone know that Yahweh would protect his city and the house that was called by his name? How blind we can be!

Shechem, Samaria, Bethel and the other towns of Israel were all conquered swiftly, and Nebuchadnezzar's army flowed on unhindered into Judah.

The owner of a peaceful country home in Judah suddenly saw an army cresting the hill behind his house. He looked down the valley for a way of escape, but saw instead another detachment of troops marching swiftly up the valley. The sunlight glinted on their spears and a trumpet sounded the attack. They broke into a run, climbing up towards him. His last hope of escape lay further up the valley where he knew a cave with a concealed entrance. Desperately he swung around, away from his home, away from his family; running, running; but as he did so, he saw for the first time the cavalry, picking their way down the valley towards him. He had no way out. There was terror on every side!

May, 589 BC – the 9th year of King Zedekiah

On the day before the army leaders predicted that King Nebuchadnezzar's army would arrive, most of the gates of the city were closed and the urgent work of filling in the empty spaces behind the gates began.

Crowds of fleeing citizens banged upon the gates to the north, east and west, but they would open for no-one. Only one gate remained open, and anyone who wanted access to the city must enter through the Valley of the Son of Hinnom. Cursed Topheth would channel the last helpless victims into the city which was to become their grave: the Valley of Slaughter, as God had called it.

The city was full to overflowing. The stores of food that had seemed ample would lessen quickly under the assault of so many extra mouths. But the violence that had been increasing over the last few years was already taking its toll among the influx of extra people. Jerusalem had become a city in which violent death would often follow even a minor insult or an accidental slight.

Not only that, but the society's expectations of worship demanded involvement in the lascivious and brutal worship of the many disgusting gods of Canaan who now claimed the allegiance of so many in Judah. Temple prostitutes and the corrupt priests of bloodthirsty idols demanded their share not only of a man's money, but also of his family, with the result that innocents died in their hundreds every week.

The reigns of Zedekiah as king and Azariah my brother as High Priest had together been the last step in Judah's total debasement.

It's not exactly a proverb, but there is a saying that some will repeat which says "Beware a weak man!" In Judah we had need of two strong men as king and high priest – men who would stand against any opposition to fulfil their responsibilities before God. Instead, the nation was being led by men who had never been appointed to any position of power at all – self-seeking friends of the king and power-hungry priests of gods who are no gods. These were the men who were wielding power in Judah, and the two appointed leaders were following.

As the gates were being reinforced with piles of compacted stones, the temple was full of worshippers – but few were worshippers of Yahweh. Women were there, weeping for Tammuz; elders were gathered, worshipping the sun between the altar and the porch; images that had been hidden in secret corners of the temple were brought out for public adulation; and painted boards like those which had lined the chamber destroyed in the time of Josiah[91] were being presented before the populace in all their disgusting detail.

Every possible part of the work of Josiah – the work that seemed to have delayed God's judgement of his people for a time – had been rolled away, and replaced with the public adoration of every evil god that had ever been worshipped in Canaan. And this in the very temple of Yahweh himself.[92]

---

[91] See 2 Kings 23:7 and Volume 2 – As Good As It Gets, Chapters 4 and 14.

[92] Jeremiah 7:30

I stood in the courts of the temple, and I shouted. I loudly condemned every part of every activity I saw – and God protected me so that I lived to tell the tale – but no-one listened! I tried to stop the repulsive worship, but crowds of people pushed me away and howled down my message. My brothers, relatives and many other priests all offered sacrifices as well, so that the supplication of a nation would rise to any deity who might listen. None would.

The temple guards supported the idolaters, and did their best to silence the few who stood in opposition.

Without question, Judah had become worse than any of the pagan nations who had lived in the promised land before them,[93] and who had been vomited out of the land because of their evil.

As God had often said to me, the approaching terror would usher in the judgement of Yahweh.

☙

Nebuchadnezzar did indeed arrive the next day, and the hordes that followed him – from all the nations he had conquered[94] – continued to arrive over the following days until the city was completely surrounded.

Those few of us who had endured the last siege during Jeconiah's brief reign settled down to endure another siege. Others watched with trepidation as engines of war were quickly set up by the surrounding armies, and once again large stones and arrows began to rain down on the city from above.

The cisterns and storehouses were all full, but the city was overfull with people. The wise suggested immediate

---

[93] 2 Kings 21:9, 11; 2 Chronicles 33:9
[94] Jeremiah 34:1

rationing, but the king's friends opposed all such constraints.

☙

August, 589 BC – the 9th year of King Zedekiah

Over the next three months, nothing special happened. The Chaldeans sat outside the city and waited, and we sat inside the city and waited.

But don't get the impression that the siege was all about waiting: attacks by units of the Chaldean army were frequent and battering rams were used on every gate around the city. The precaution of packing the space behind each gate with stones had worked well so far, and none of the gates had been broken down. Frequent night-time raids by both sides guaranteed that neither side slept without guards, and occasional daring raids from within the city kept the Chaldeans on their toes when they were manoeuvring equipment near the walls.

Nevertheless, everyone seemed to be settling down into an easy routine that helped to sustain the confidence of Zedekiah's advisors: Jerusalem could endure another siege without the need for a foolish surrender such as Jeconiah had made.

God's words burned within me every day and drove me to do my best to convince the city that God's judgement was coming – but it didn't seem to achieve much. I had more than enough words from God to work with, after all, he had been warning of what would come since the thirteenth year of Josiah – but few would ever listen.

Then, one day, as I finished speaking to an uncaring crowd near the palace gate, the burning urge to speak – which often subsided for a while after I had spoken God's words – began instead to increase.

The feeling of flames consuming me from within quickly became strong enough to cause me physical pain, and I fell to my knees, gasping. I looked up desperately towards heaven and seemed to see flames all around me: flames of the city burning. The pain continued to increase until suddenly the voice of God spoke from heaven, above the flames. Apparently no-one else heard the voice, but the words were loud and strong in my ears:

"Thus says the Lord, the God of Israel:
Go and speak to Zedekiah king of Judah
and say to him, 'Thus says the Lord:
Behold, I am giving this city
into the hand of the king of Babylon,
and he shall burn it with fire.
You shall not escape from his hand
but shall surely be captured and delivered into his hand.
You shall see the king of Babylon eye to eye
and speak with him face to face.
And you shall go to Babylon.'
Yet hear the word of the Lord,
O Zedekiah king of Judah!
Thus says the Lord concerning you:
'You shall not die by the sword.
You shall die in peace.
And as spices were burned for your fathers,
the former kings who were before you,
so people shall burn spices for you
and lament for you, saying, "Alas, lord!" '
For I have spoken the word, declares the Lord."[95]

As the voice spoke, the flames within me gradually died down a little and the pain receded. When God's words finished, I immediately stood up and marched to the gates of the palace, telling the guards that I must speak with the king urgently. Within a very short time, I was led

---

[95] Jeremiah 34:2-5

into the palace, down a corridor, and into a side room that I had never entered before. King Zedekiah was reclining at a table, nibbling a fig.

"Jeremiah," said Zedekiah, casually, "I hear that you have an urgent message. Is it good news?"

"No, my lord," I replied, "it is not good news. What good news can there be when you and your friends continue to ignore every word God has spoken to you?"

"That's not fair!" he objected, sitting up straight. "I have spoken to you quite a few times, and treated you with great respect. If I did what my friends suggested, you would never even get to talk to me at all!"

"Anyway," I continued, "Yahweh has just told me to give you this message." Without waiting for his response, whatever it might be, I began to recite the words of God, warning first of destruction by fire and then of his captivity and death.

As usual, Zedekiah listened carefully, and when I finished, he looked a little nonplussed. "Compared with what happened to my brother Jehoiakim, that is almost good news, Jeremiah," he mused. "But why is God so determined to destroy Jerusalem?"

"Have you ever obeyed his commands?" I asked. "The whole nation loves false gods and listens to false prophets in preference to the real God." As I spoke, some words God had spoken long before glowed on the wall in my mind, standing out brilliantly and demanding that I repeat them:

"For if you truly amend your ways and your deeds,
　　if you truly execute justice one with another,
　if you do not oppress the sojourner, the fatherless,
　or the widow, or shed innocent blood in this place,
and if you do not go after other gods to your own harm,
　then I will let you dwell in this place, in the land

that I gave of old to your fathers forever.
"Behold, you trust in deceptive words to no avail."[96]

Once again, the king listened carefully before sighing. "Well, I'll think about what we can do," he said, and that was the end of my interview.

☙

Zedekiah definitely thought – as he had said he would. It was more than I had expected.

Shortly after our discussion, news spread from the palace that King Zedekiah had convinced the rich people in Jerusalem that judgement would be sure to come upon them in the siege if they did not make some concessions to Yahweh's laws.

After negotiations, it was agreed that all Hebrews in the city would be proclaimed free. Anyone who owned a Hebrew slave, whether male or female, would set them free, and no-one would enslave a Jew, his brother.[97]

I remember it well as a time of joy. I was joyful because finally the king had listened to God's words and was taking some steps towards repentance. I also knew some of the people in the city who were slaves and was glad for their sakes.

My other reason for joy was that my brother was also involved in the matter. He organised a formal ceremony where a covenant could be cut with God.[98] Partly following the example that God set so long ago with Abraham,[99] a calf was to be cut in half and the slave owners would walk between the two parts of the calf to

---

[96] Jeremiah 7:5-8
[97] Jeremiah 34:8-9
[98] The Hebrew word for "covenant" has overtones of cutting, probably because animals were commonly cut in two when making a covenant.
[99] Genesis 15:7-21

show their commitment to the promise they were making. Azariah arranged the entire ceremony, a serious ritual that would bring together all those who owned a Hebrew as a slave and express appropriate thankfulness for their generosity in proclaiming freedom for all.

Late on the selected afternoon, when the besieging Chaldeans were conveniently quiet, the calf was led out to stand patiently near the large altar in the courts of the temple. A large group of men – all those who owned Hebrew slaves – stood nearby waiting for their turn to shine as generous and godly citizens. Many had very little experience with worship in Yahweh's temple, and several priests were on hand to give instructions as necessary. A large crowd surrounded the group; these were the slaves whose freedom was being promised in a covenant made in the name of Yahweh before many witnesses.

My brother carried the knife and swiftly cut the calf's throat, starting the blood draining into a bowl. Levites caught the calf as it collapsed, and soon it had been carefully cut in two. One part was left where it had been slaughtered, while the other was carried to one side to leave a pathway between the halves.

One after another, the rich slave-owners walked between the pieces of the unfortunate calf,[100] and as each one passed, a cheer arose from the watching crowd and smiles broke out on many faces.

Many officials of Judah and Jerusalem, some of the king's eunuchs, several of the priests and various other people of the land passed between the parts of the calf.[101] When the solemn ceremony concluded, the king's demand had been met and all of the Hebrew slaves had been freed. Their erstwhile owners hoped that the generosity they were being compelled to show would be

---

[100] Jeremiah 34:18
[101] Jeremiah 34:19

worthwhile. Nebuchadnezzar's army out beyond the walls was an ever-threatening sight, and any celestial assistance that could be obtained in the conflict would be appreciated.

It was a day of great joy for the slaves whose freedom had been guaranteed before God.

℃

October, 589 BC – the 9th year of King Zedekiah

I suppose that seven weeks of freedom were better than none, but for the slaves who were quickly rounded up and pressed into slavery again, there was little to rejoice about.

It was a series of events that a knowledge of human greed should have made predictable, but it still came as a shock to me.

First came the news that Pharaoh had responded to Zedekiah's urgent request for help. A large army, it was said, had crossed the Brook of Egypt and was camped on the coast, ready to march on Jerusalem.

Nebuchadnezzar's response was swift. Within three days, there was not a single Chaldean soldier left within sight of Jerusalem: all had marched towards the coast, ready to meet the army of Egypt.

A feeling of boundless relief spread through the city, and impromptu parties of celebration sprang up everywhere.

Over the next few days, scouts brought the news of a standoff at the southern border: two armies camped opposite each other, each looking for the advantage of a better position, but neither willing to commit to open battle. Weeks passed and the tension in the city gradually eased. The thoughts of the rich naturally turned again to business, and it was then that their pious commitments and much-lauded generosity became a liability – to be abandoned without scruple. Within days, the former slaves had all been gathered together and handed back to their old masters. Resistance was useless, for the power was on the side of the rich as usual, and not the faintest twinge of conscience seemed to affect these oath-breakers.

Chapter 15

Retribution

God's response to the unfaithfulness of the rich was also swift – although still only in words at that point.

People ask me from time to time why God cares whether we keep or break our oaths. Of course, I cannot answer for God specifically, but our scriptures show clearly that God cares deeply about faithfulness and honesty. When he makes covenants with people he always keeps them, so it should be no surprise when he is angry about people who are covenant-breakers and oath-breakers.

Yahweh is a God of truth and faithfulness.

It was only two days after they started rounding up the freed slaves and handing them back to their former owners that God spoke to me at night. His words were not gentle, and the anger with which they were delivered felt broad enough to fill the whole city.

Before I repeat what he said, I should try to explain a little how it feels to receive God's messages and the emotion that they have often conveyed, particularly in later times. Whenever God speaks to me in anger at my people, my immediate reaction is a feeling of guilt: "What," I ask myself, often in terror, "have I done wrong?" Then, once God's words make it clear that his anger is not aimed specifically at me, there is a great feeling of relief and very little immediate feeling of sympathy for those who are the target of his anger. Yet his anger is never the sort that men show, an anger that results in a loss of control and the saying of thoughtless words. No, the anger that pervades God's words is carefully explained by the words themselves.

Of that night, all I can say is that God's anger prompted my normal response. He began:

> "Thus says the Lord, the God of Israel:
> I myself made a covenant with your fathers
> when I brought them out of the land of Egypt,
> out of the house of slavery, saying,
> 'At the end of seven years each of you must
> set free the fellow Hebrew who has been sold to you
> and has served you six years;
> you must set him free from your service.'
> But your fathers did not listen to me
> or incline their ears to me."[102]

In just a few words, God had pointed out the covenant that he had made with Israel regarding the treatment of servants. It had been based on the fact that he had freed them from Egypt, and that they were not allowed to enslave each other. As usual, our fathers had taken advantage of the gift of freedom that God had offered, but ignored the commitments they had made in return. Most of the rich people in Jerusalem were newly rich. Riches had come to them only after so many had been taken into exile at the time when Zedekiah had been made king. They had revelled in the new opportunities available

---

[102] Jeremiah 34:13-14

in a kingdom from which most of the successful people had been removed. In rising in the world, they had taken the position of the oppressing rich. They had taken advantage of those who remained poor and forced them first into service, then into slavery. Now that they themselves were in a position of power, their earlier complaints about slavery were no longer heard, and the seventh year, the year of freedom, had passed without any slaves being freed.

Zedekiah had initiated the freeing of the slaves, and for once, the slight feeling of guilt they felt over flouting the historic laws of Judah had combined with their superstitious fears to prompt them to free their brothers – as they ought to have done without any prompting.

Yet God still had more to say, in the beautifully concise manner he normally uses:

> "You recently repented
> and did what was right in my eyes
> by proclaiming liberty, each to his neighbour,
> and you made a covenant before me
> in the house that is called by my name,
> but then you turned around and profaned my name
> when each of you took back his male and female slaves,
> whom you had set free according to their desire,
> and you brought them into subjection
> to be your slaves."[103]

As usual, the absolute minimum of words required to describe what had happened and to express God's opinion of it. How it cuts me to the heart whenever God explains that our breaking of oaths we have made in his name sullies his name and makes it unclean! The knowledge is almost unbearable. Yet God's words were matter of fact

---

[103] Jeremiah 34:15-16

enough, even as they described a condemnation that would prove anything but matter of fact:

"Therefore, thus says the Lord:
You have not obeyed me by proclaiming liberty,
every one to his brother and to his neighbour;
behold, I proclaim to you liberty to the sword,
to pestilence, and to famine, declares the Lord.
I will make you a horror to all the kingdoms of the earth.
And the men who transgressed my covenant
and did not keep the terms of the covenant
that they made before me,
I will make them like the calf
that they cut in two and passed between its parts –
the officials of Judah, the officials of Jerusalem,
the eunuchs, the priests, and all the people of the land
who passed between the parts of the calf.
And I will give them into the hand of their enemies
and into the hand of those who seek their lives.
Their dead bodies shall be food for the birds of the air
and the beasts of the earth."[104]

As I listened to Yahweh's words and pictured the people whom I had witnessed walking between the pieces of the calf, I saw also pictures of Topheth, which God had named "The Valley of Slaughter". There, I seemed to see the disembowelled bodies of these men, treated with as little care and sympathy as they had shown to the calf which had died when they formed a covenant that had been carelessly cast aside as soon as it became inconvenient. So these men would die as menaces for whom God's time of tolerance had passed.

But God was not yet finished, instead promising the devastating return of Nebuchadnezzar's besieging army:

"And Zedekiah king of Judah and his officials
I will give into the hand of their enemies

---

[104] Jeremiah 34:17-20

and into the hand of those who seek their lives,
into the hand of the army of the king of Babylon
which has withdrawn from you.
Behold, I will command, declares the Lord,
and will bring them back to this city.
And they will fight against it
and take it and burn it with fire.
I will make the cities of Judah
a desolation without inhabitant."[105]

I remained awake that night long after the voice had ceased and the feeling of God's anger had abated somewhat. The feeling of anger did not go completely, but God's anger mixed with my own. I thought of the harshness of men who would promise freedom and then snatch it away again because it suited them to do so – and because they felt that deliverance had come by the hand of Pharaoh. Repentance and obedience could only find a place in their hearts when they felt threatened themselves; they were not genuine. No compassion or sympathy had softened their hearts, only a lurking fear that they might suffer if they did not demonstrate some level of fairness. When Nebuchadnezzar had marched away, the terror that had surrounded them had gone with him, leaving their true colours showing again.

No wonder God was furious with such hypocrites! Nevertheless, I also mulled over the justice of his judgement and the implications of his words. How would God balance his judgement of these men with the freedom that should have been given to their slaves? Would everyone in the city suffer because of the unfaithfulness of the slave owners or would their punishments be individually targeted?

---

[105] Jeremiah 34:21-22

❦

King Zedekiah received the denouncement of the slave owners with something like resignation. He had already heard God's condemnation of oath-breakers: his own behaviour in breaking his oath by rebelling against King Nebuchadnezzar had earned him God's condemnation, delivered through more than one prophet.

Back in the seventh year of Zedekiah's reign, an unexpected letter had arrived for the king, sent from somewhere near Babylon. But it was not one of the series of letters from King Nebuchadnezzar that had alternately threatened and cajoled ever since Zedekiah's rebellion had become known in Babylon. Instead, it was from a man who claimed to be a prophet of God, and one whom I knew personally – although not particularly well.

It was from Ezekiel,[106] the young priest who had shown such a yearning for a close relationship with God and had been taken into exile at the same time as Jeconiah. He must have continued to pursue his goal of godliness while in exile, and apparently God had spoken to him in the land of Chaldea.

His message was no message of encouragement for King Zedekiah, but rather a parable of eagles and a vine. I had a chance to read the parable because Zedekiah sent some representatives to ask me if I had prompted Ezekiel to send the letter. I hadn't, but I was very pleased to see it all the same, as it confirmed just how important Zedekiah's breach of faith was in God's eyes. Some of the words were:

---

[106] There is no evidence that Ezekiel reported his visions to anyone in Judah; however, in Ezekiel 17:2, he was told to speak the parable to the house of Israel, whereas on another occasion he was told to go and speak to the exiles (Ezekiel 3:11).

"As I live, declares the Lord God,
surely in the place where the king dwells
who made him king, whose oath he despised,
and whose covenant with him he broke,
in Babylon he shall die.
Pharaoh with his mighty army and great company
will not help him in war, when mounds are cast up
and siege walls built to cut off many lives.
He despised the oath in breaking the covenant,
and behold, he gave his hand and did all these things;
he shall not escape.
Therefore thus says the Lord God:
As I live, surely it is my oath that he despised,
and my covenant that he broke.
I will return it upon his head.
I will spread my net over him,
and he shall be taken in my snare,
and I will bring him to Babylon
and enter into judgment with him there
for the treachery he has committed against me."[107]

Unfortunately, I suspected that in the intervening two years, Zedekiah had forgotten the warning that Pharaoh's help would be useless. Or maybe he had just completely ignored the letter.

ℭℛ

November, 589 BC – the 9th year of King Zedekiah

Zedekiah didn't give up. He kept asking for God's mercy, although he refused to do anything that indicated any sort of repentance for his oath-breaking or that of his officials.

---

[107] Ezekiel 17:16-20

Not long after God had given his message against those who had forced their Hebrew servants back into slavery, King Zedekiah sent to me Jehucal the son of Shelemiah, and Zephaniah the priest, the son of Maaseiah. As a priest, I knew Zephaniah quite well, but I knew little of Jehucal. When I greeted them at my door, neither of them seemed very much at ease.

"Greetings," I said, looking from one to the other, wondering what they had come for.

"Ah, greetings, Jeremiah," said Zephaniah slowly. "King Zedekiah has sent us to you. Jehucal will explain what the king wants."

Jehucal looked at Zephaniah as if he wasn't keen to do the explaining either. "Yes, indeed," he said abruptly – almost rudely – "the king's request – well, I'm sure Zephaniah is the best person to explain it, since it is a religious matter."

"Oh, I suppose so," replied Zephaniah tersely, and then blurted out, "The king says, 'Please pray for us to the Lord our God.' "[108]

Suddenly their reluctance made sense! Having to come to me – a critic of all officials and a perceived rebel against the priesthood – would have upset both of them greatly, and probably made them feel subordinated to me in some way. No wonder they had each wanted the other to declare their errand!

I explained to them that God had forbidden me from praying to intercede for my nation,[109] but that I could inquire of Yahweh if that was all they were asking me to do. As I spoke these words, God provided me with a reply to pass on to them:

---

[108] Jeremiah 37:3
[109] Jeremiah 7:16; 11:14; 14:11

"Thus says the Lord, God of Israel:
Thus shall you say to the king of Judah
who sent you to me to inquire of me,
'Behold, Pharaoh's army that came to help you
is about to return to Egypt, to its own land.
And the Chaldeans shall come back
and fight against this city.
They shall capture it and burn it with fire.
Thus says the Lord, Do not deceive yourselves,
saying, "The Chaldeans will surely go away from us,"
for they will not go away.
For even if you should defeat
the whole army of Chaldeans
who are fighting against you,
and there remained of them only wounded men,
every man in his tent,
they would rise up and burn this city with fire.' "[110]

This message dashed all of the hopes and wishes of the leaders, and I couldn't help contrasting the entire situation with the time in Josiah's eighteenth year when he had sent messengers – more in number and more important – to see whether the curses in the Book of the Law could be avoided by any means. Josiah had sent the High Priest and his most senior official; Zedekiah had sent the priest who was second in command[111] and one other official of no particularly important rank. For Josiah, sending that delegation had been a matter of paramount importance. For Zedekiah, it was not completely unimportant, but the personnel he chose seemed to reveal a lower priority.

Jehucal was in a hurry to leave and throughout the interview had seemed to find it hard to be civil to me. It

---

[110] Jeremiah 37:7-10

[111] Two years later in Jeremiah 52:24, Zephaniah is said to be the second most important priest.

was not until some time later that I thought further about Jehucal and his family. Jehucal was the son of Shelemiah, and that name was to prove important. Enemies can arise from many quarters, and relatives can be vengeful.

Three weeks later, the news reached Jerusalem that Pharaoh's army had withdrawn from the confrontation with Nebuchadnezzar. It was not a complete capitulation, but it was clear that Pharaoh would not be giving any of the support that Zedekiah had requested.

Zedekiah was on his own. Nebuchadnezzar would soon be back at the walls of Jerusalem.

In the meantime, I planned to take advantage of our temporary freedom from siege to visit Anathoth. Several of the priests in Anathoth had been killed during the advance of the Chaldean army, and as a result, I and my brothers had each inherited some land from a distant uncle. Given God's prophecies, the deaths of these men were no surprise to me, but they still made me sad. As for my inheritance – the land was probably worth nothing in the current situation, but I still decided to go and look at it and register my acceptance of the property. I felt it was best to get the matter finalised quickly.

It was a cold, grey morning that threatened rain as I went to the Benjamin Gate. I was walking past the guards there when a sentry named Irijah the son of Shelemiah approached, with a hostile look in his eye.

"What are you doing, Jeremiah?" he asked, aggressively.

"I'm going out to Anathoth to receive some land that I have inherited," I replied, calmly, wondering why he seemed so agitated.

"Oh, yes! Valuable land, I suppose," sneered Irijah.

"Let me guess, you're going out to inspect it and are planning to sell it for a fortune just before the Chaldeans return!"

"I'm going to inspect it and finalise the paperwork," I responded, still trying to remain calm.

"Nobody would bother doing that now – the land is worth nothing. You're deserting to the Chaldeans."[112]

"It's a lie," I protested, "I am not deserting to the Chaldeans."[113]

But Irijah would not listen. He was much younger than I, and stronger too, so it didn't take him long to get a rope around my neck and drag me into one of the chambers near the gate, where some of the senior officials were hearing legal cases.[114]

He barged in with all the angry authority of a guard who has permission to interrupt less important hearings when the security of the city is at stake.

"Excuse me, sir," he said to the chief of the officials, "sorry to interrupt and all that, but this prophet" – he almost spat out the word – "this prophet Jeremiah is trying to desert to the Chaldeans."

"Deserting, eh? That's a serious crime," responded the official, looking at me with distaste. "I always thought Jeremiah was a traitor, anyway." Turning back to Irijah, he said, "Now, you are Irijah, aren't you? Jehucal's brother?"

"Yes, sir," he answered, proudly, "Irijah the son of Shelemiah, son of Hananiah."[115] He glanced across at me with disdain, then continued, "And I'm sure that he's a traitor, sir. He should be beaten and locked up." Then

---

112 Jeremiah 37:13
113 Jeremiah 37:14
114 Jeremiah 37:14
115 Jeremiah 37:13

he looked at me in a considering way and smiled vindictively, saying, "Or maybe it warrants even more serious punishment, sir."

Suddenly it struck me: Irijah and Jehucal; both were grandsons of Hananiah, the false prophet whom God had killed five years earlier because of his false prophesying! What mercy could I hope for from either of them?

Chapter 16

Imprisoned

Mercy certainly didn't come into it.

They called it a hearing, but there didn't seem to be any listening going on. Jehucal, Shephatiah, Pashhur and a few others of Zedekiah's officials got together and asked Irijah what had happened. He reported his lies as fact and they believed every word he said. No-one asked me any questions, or listened when I reminded them of the penalties the law specified for those who bore false witness.

So I was beaten again and taken to the house of Jonathan the scribe, which had been converted into a prison. The city was still rather crowded at that stage, and the officials wanted a place where they could put prisoners without having to tell Zedekiah. Below-ground there were vaulted chambers with rooms leading off them that had once been used by scribes making copies of important documents for the king. These rooms had been turned into dark dungeons, and it was into one of these that I was thrown.

As I lay in the darkness for days, I wondered who would know where I was. My mother lived in my home: she needed my help, but would she know where I was? Were the officials gloating publicly over my imprisonment, or was I just one of the many people who had silently disappeared in this city of violence? Would Azariah hear of my fate from the officials? I believed that he already spent far too much time with them, sharing in their wickedness – but would they merely keep him as their ignorant puppet?

Would even King Zedekiah know where I was? – and would he care anyway?

My back slowly recovered from the beating, but the winter was terribly cold and my jailers made little effort to care for me. Meals were sporadic and I was given very little opportunity to see the sun. I had plenty of time for prayer as I sat alone in the blackness, but no chance to watch the sun rise or set, or even to see God's creation around me. It was a dark and difficult time.

☙

"I feel as if I should know you," I said, shaking my head.

"Well, I don't know you at all," he replied impatiently, speaking with an accent from the north of Israel. "Who are you anyway?"

"I'm Jeremiah, the son of Hilkiah," I answered. "What's your name?"

He showed no sign of recognising my name, but responded, with an air of suspicion, "In my line of business, we're not that eager to spout our names."

"What is your line of business?"

"Don't ask," he said, shaking his head. "Look, how about we just forget about this conversation? I don't know you, you don't know me, and you don't know my line of business either. That's the best way to leave it."

That seemed like the end of my investigation, but my mind doesn't like letting go of unanswered questions. I had seen this man on a few occasions during my stay in the house of Jonathan the scribe. Most of my time was spent underground in the cells, but occasionally they had let me out briefly to see the sun, and it was during those periods that I had seen him. Right from when I first saw him, a faint feeling of recognition had troubled me, but I had never before been allowed to approach him. Each time he had been sitting morosely, chained up in one corner of the small walled courtyard, its mosaic pavement surrounding a central pool, now empty of water.

On this occasion, however, he was working, clearing leaves and dirt from the pool area, and I had jumped at the chance to speak to him – unsuccessfully as yet.

I decided to have one last try: "Did I meet you up in the north of Israel?"

His reaction was immediate: "No, I've never been in the north of Israel."

Was he lying? His accent proclaimed him a northerner, yet he was flatly denying ever having gone there. I really couldn't let the subject go!

"Where do you come from, then?" I asked.

Amazingly, he named the very village that was nearest Shobai's ancestral farm.

"Ah, yes, I know the place," I said, enthusiastically. He looked a little unsure – clearly he had not expected me to know that tiny hamlet.

His accent was not the same as Shobai's and I was fairly sure he did not really come from that area. I was determined to find out more.

"Do you know a man from there called Shobai?" I asked.

"Oh… yes," he replied slowly; "at least, I know *of* him, I don't really know him."

"How was he when you saw him last?"

"I don't meet him often, but he seemed alright."

"When was that? And when did you come here?"

"Maybe a year ago. A few months before I came here, I guess," he said.

Here was the proof I wanted. I knew that Shobai had died about five years before, yet this man was claiming to have met him in the last year. So who was he, and why did he look slightly familiar?

"How did you end up in here?" I asked. "You must have powerful enemies."

"Yes, you're right," he said sadly. "Gedaliah the son of Pashhur locked me up in here shortly after I arrived in Jerusalem. You know how crowded the city was when the siege started? Well, I had nowhere to stay, so I found my way into an empty house, but when I got in I discovered that it wasn't empty. Quite a few refugees like me had been staying there for a while – we had nowhere else to live. Then one night, this Gedaliah came along with soldiers and arrested us all. Apparently the house was his and he didn't want anyone using it. I think they let everybody else go, after ordering them to find somewhere else to stay, and I suppose that I would have been alright too if I hadn't said what I thought of someone who chose to keep their house empty while hundreds or thousands of people in the city had nowhere to live. He didn't like that! But I don't have much of an opinion of filthy rich people. I'm all for evening up the spread of wealth," he concluded.

There, I had it! Now I knew where I had met him. His words had given me the clues I needed.

"What happened to your friend Zimri, Nathan?" I asked, casually.

His eyes opened wide and his mouth did too. He was so shocked that he didn't even try to pretend that he didn't know what I was talking about.

"Zimri wasn't my *friend*, just one of the gang," he said. "He was killed years ago, just after Jehoiakim became king. He was always getting into fights, and one day he didn't see the knife in his opponent's left hand. No loss, really."

"Did you find someone to replace Pelet?"

Nathan tipped his head on one side and stared at me for a moment, then a glimmer of recognition showed. "Now I remember you," he said. "You were that man I met on the road up north, the one who lectured me about God's rules. I never could work out why I stopped Zimri from killing you. He wanted to, you know."

Back in the time of Josiah, I had travelled into Israel for a while and delivered God's messages to any audience I could find.[116] Nathan had been a young man then, and had tried to recruit me into a gang of robbers, but had chosen to protect me from his truculent partner, Zimri, when I had refused.

"What have you done since then, Nathan?" I asked.

"I've spent my life on the roads, doing my best to make rich people suffer."

"And what brought you to Jerusalem?"

"We lived out in the country and had our own safe places to stay, but once Nebuchadnezzar's army came, there was nowhere left to hide. When the Chaldeans

---

[116] See Volume 1 – Early Days, Chapter 16

came before, during Jehoiakim's reign and again in Jeconiah's reign, it wasn't hard to hide. But this time was different. They seemed to cover the whole land. All of our secret hiding places were being overrun. Soldiers seemed to fill the roads day and night. We had to hurry to keep ahead of them." He laughed hollowly. "You may have thought that *we* were dangerous, but they killed a lot more people than we ever did. Men and women, young and old – anyone and everyone they met, it seemed. At one stage, we ended up behind their front lines for a few days. We had to split up, and it took all my skill to stay unseen until I was able to get ahead of them again. I've never seen more bodies than I saw during those few days. A lot more dead people than living ones, I can tell you – dead *and* mutilated. That was what convinced me to head for Jerusalem as quickly as I could. I had actually planned to keep going further south, but I hurt my knee one day when I had to drop suddenly behind a wall and landed on a sharp stone. By the time I got here, I could hardly walk."

"How was life in the north before Nebuchadnezzar came?" I asked.

"Hard. There was no easy living, even for us."

"What about religion? Josiah cleaned up much of the worship of idols, and encouraged people to serve Yahweh. Did any of his reforms last?"

"No – within a year of Josiah's death, Israel had just as many altars to just as many idols as there had ever been before. I don't really care much about religion, but everyone knows that trying to make our nation serve Yahweh has never had a chance. We're a stubborn nation, you know, and I've never seen that stubbornness being used for good. It's funny, you know – those cursed foreigners that the Assyrians dumped in our land care more about Yahweh than we natives do!"

CR

The cold and darkness left my cell reluctantly. My health had been bad all winter – I seemed to go from one sickness to the next without a break. I'm sure that being cold all of the time didn't help.

Even when the weather gradually warmed, my normal energy and enthusiasm did not return. I began to wonder whether I would die in that place.

My jailers told me almost nothing about what was happening in the city and refused to answer any of my questions. From time to time, though, I was able to talk to Nathan, and I learned much from him about the terror that the Chaldeans had brought to the land. God's prophecies of terror on every side had certainly come true. No doubt the terror would eventually fill Jerusalem too. But would I live to see it?

As spring passed and I began to feel genuinely warm at times, my jailers let slip one item of news that I was clearly not meant to learn: Nebuchadnezzar and his army had returned just as God had predicted. I didn't hear the details until later, but apparently about a month after I had been put in the dungeon, Nebuchadnezzar had led his men back up from the south to encircle the walls of Jerusalem once more. Jerusalem had his full attention and would regret every bit of it.

Shortly after that news slipped out, the jailers brought me another piece of news, and this time they were eager to tell me: the High Priest Azariah, my brother, was dead.

Free Download

Paul in Snippets

A 109-page PDF novelette by Mark Morgan.

The life of Paul painted from the Acts of the Apostles.

Get your free copy of *Paul in Snippets* when you sign up for the Bible Tales mailing list. As well as the eBook, you will receive a weekly email newsletter with micro tales, informative articles and special offers.

Visit **http://www.BibleTales.online/free-pins**

www.BibleTales.online

Bible Tales Online

Other books by Mark Morgan are available from Bible Tales Online.

Terror on Every Side!

THE LIFE OF JEREMIAH

From a family of priests in the peaceful reign of good King Josiah, came a young man Jeremiah, bringing words from God to his people. It was no message for the fainthearted, either. It was a message of *Terror on Every Side!*

Volume 1 – Early Days
Volume 2 – As Good As It Gets
Volume 3 – Darkness Falling
Volume 4 – The Darkness Deepens
Volume 5 – No Remedy

Generally available as paperback, eBook and audiobook.

Micro-tales

Collections of short stories about Bible characters or events, available in paperback, eBook and audiobook.

Fiction Favours the Facts
Fiction Favours the Facts – Book 2

Other novels

Joseph, Rachel's son

Bible Tales Online continues to publish books.
To find the list of currently available books, visit

http://www.BibleTales.online/books

www.BibleTales.online

www.ingramcontent.com/pod-product-compliance
Lightning Source LLC
Chambersburg PA
CBHW070940190726
48292CB00004B/1272